SECOND CHANCE WITH LORD BRANSCOMBE

BY
JOANNA NEIL

MILLS & BOON

First published in Great Britain 2016 By Mills & Boon, an imprint of HarperCollins Publishers 1 London Bridge Street, London, SE1 9GF

Large Print edition 2017

© 2016 Joanna Neil

ISBN: 978-0-263-06694-4

Printed and bound in Great Britain by CPI Antony Rowe, Chippenham, Wiltshire

Joanna Neil loves writing romance and has written more than sixty books for Mills & Boon. Before her writing career started she had a variety of jobs, which included being a telephonist and a clerk, as well as nursing and work in a hospital pharmacy. She was an infant teacher for a number of years before her love of writing took over. Her hobbies include dressmaking, cooking and gardening.

Books by Joanna Neil

Mills & Boon Medical Romance

Dr Right All Along
Tamed by Her Brooding Boss
His Bride in Paradise
Return of the Rebel Doctor
Sheltered by Her Top-Notch Boss
A Doctor to Remember
Daring to Date Her Boss
Temptation in Paradise
Resisting Her Rebel Doc
Her Holiday Miracle

Visit the Author Profile page at millsandboon.co.uk for more titles.

For my family,
with thanks for their unfailing love
and support through the years.

**Praise for
Joanna Neil**

'…a well-written romance set in the
beautiful Caribbean.'

—Harlequin Junkie on
Temptation in Paradise

'I really enjoyed this read. Sometimes the
tension between Matt and Saffi was simply
crackling… If you enjoy Medicals this is a
good, solid read…well worth it.'

—Harlequin Junkie on
A Doctor to Remember

Lincolnshire
COUNTY COUNCIL
Working for a better future

discover libraries
This book should be returned on or before the due date.

04/17   NEI

To renew or order library books please telephone 01522 782010
or visit https://lincolnshirespydus.co.uk
You will require a Personal Identification Number
Ask any member of staff for this.
The above does not apply to Reader's Group Collection Stock.

EC. 199 (LIBS): RS/L5/19

Nate slipped his arm around her waist, holding her close.

She knew she ought to move away, but it felt good to have him hold her—to have him so close that she could feel his long body by her side—and she couldn't bring herself to break that contact. Instead, Sophie wanted him to wrap his arms around her. His nearness was intoxicating.

'You're lovely,' he said huskily, his gaze lingering on the pink fullness of her mouth. 'It means so much to me to have you here with me like this. I've missed you all these years we've been away from each other. I kept thinking about you all the time we were apart.'

'Did you? Me too...'

It was true. She'd never been able to stop thinking about him. And now she was lost in his spell, enticed by the compelling lure of his dark eyes and mesmerised by the gentle sweep of his hands as they moved over the curve of her hips, drawing her ever closer to him.

He bent his head to her and gently claimed her lips, brushing her mouth softly with his kisses. Her whole body seemed to turn to flame and she melted into his embrace, loving the way his arms went around her. Her limbs were weak with longing. She wanted his kisses...yearned to know the feel of his hands moving over her.

Dear Reader,

I've always loved coastal settings, and this book has one of my favourites—an English Devonshire village clustered around a sheltered bay. At the centre of this community is the Manor House and its estate, overlooking all—the proud heritage of the Branscombe family through generations. What could be a better, more perfect background for an enduring love story?

But, as you know, the path of true love never runs smooth, and Nate and Sophie have more than their fair share of troubles. How can their love survive the hostility that simmers between their fathers? Or overcome the overwhelming problems that cascade down upon Nate's head?

It takes a special kind of man to win against all the odds—and I hope you'll agree with me that Sophie deserves the best!

Happy reading.

With love,

Joanna

CHAPTER ONE

'IT'S BEAUTIFUL OUT HERE, isn't it?' Jake smiled as he looked out over the sea and watched the waves rolling on to the shore. 'I never get tired of looking at that glorious view. I'm just glad I get the chance to come and sit here after work sometimes.'

'Me too.' Sophie returned the smile and then concentrated on carefully spooning golden sugar crystals into her coffee. It gave her a bit of time to think. She *ought* to be content, no doubt about it, but she couldn't get rid of this nagging feeling that before too long everything in her world was going to be turned upside down.

On the surface everything was running smoothly. What could be better than to be here on a late Friday afternoon, taking in the fresh sea air with Jake, on the terrace of this restaurant in the delightful little fishing village they called home? On the North Devon coast, a small inlet in a wide bay, it was an idyllic place to live.

A faint warm breeze was blowing in off the blue water, riffling gently through her long honey-blonde curls and lightly fanning her cheeks. From here she could see the rocky crags that enclosed the peaceful cove and she could hear the happy shouts of children playing on the beach below, dipping their nets into rock pools that had been left behind by the outgoing tide. She had every reason to be happy.

The truth was, though, that she'd been on edge this last couple of weeks...and there could be only one reason for that. Ever since Nate Branscombe had returned to the Manor House her emotions had been on a roller-coaster ride. Maybe she should have expected him to come back once he'd heard about his father's health taking a downward turn. Deep down, she'd known all along he would have to visit his father, Lord Branscombe, sooner or later, but when she'd heard he'd actually turned up she'd been swamped by a feeling akin to panic. She'd gone out of her way since then to avoid running into him.

'This is the perfect place to relax,' Jake said, oblivious to her subdued mood. He sipped his coffee and then glanced at his watch. 'I can't stay for too much longer, though…much as I'd like to—I have a meeting to go to.'

'Ah—the joys of working in hospital management!' She glanced at him, her mouth crinkling at the corners. It was what he was born to do, streamlining what went on in various departments of the local hospital.

Jake Holdsworth was a clever, likeable young man, good-looking, with neat dark hair and compassionate brown eyes. He was a couple of years older than her at twenty-eight, but they'd known each other for several years since he used to regularly come to the village to visit a favourite aunt. They'd become firm friends. Eventually, though, they'd gone their separate ways when they each left home to take up places at university—she went to Medical School and Jake went off to study Hospital and Health Services Management. It was one of her proudest moments when she was at last able to call herself Dr Trent.

'Oh, yes! Budget meetings, purchasing committees, dealing with the complaints of clinicians! It's all go!'

'But you love it.' Their lives had been busy, as each of them worked towards building their careers, and it was only lately they'd met up again. Jake had a keen sense of humour and she liked spending time with him. He always managed to put her at ease, to help her set aside her troubled family situation for a while, to make her forget that life could be a struggle sometimes. He was a restful kind of man and she enjoyed talking to him.

He was nothing at all like Nate Branscombe— the very opposite, in fact. She frowned. Somehow, Nate had the knack of stirring up strong passions in her—for good or bad—but, either way, they were feelings she would far sooner forget. More often than not, he left her in turmoil.

Nate had the kind of bone-melting good looks that sent her heart into overdrive the moment she saw him. Women couldn't get enough of him but, as far as he was concerned, it was all easy come, easy go. His girlfriends each thought they would be the one to change him, but she could have told them they were wasting their time. He would never make that final commitment.

Maybe that was why Sophie had always held back from him. He wanted her, there had been no doubt about it, and she'd been so…so…tempted, but she wasn't going to fall for him, like all the others, and end up being hurt. Nate liked women, enjoyed being with them, having fun, getting the most out of life, but she wondered if he'd ever meet the woman who was right for him. Or maybe Nate was aware that the women he'd dated simply didn't make the grade to be the wife of a future lord.

'Are you okay? You're a bit quiet today.' Jake studied her thoughtfully. 'Have you had a tough day at the hospital?'

'Oh—I'm sorry. I was miles away.' Jerked out of her reverie, Sophie made an effort to pull herself together. 'No, it was fine.'

'Is it some problem closer to home, then? Are you worried about your family?' Jake gave her a wry, coaxing smile before finishing off his coffee and resting his hands on the table, his fingers loosely clasped.

She shrugged her shoulders. 'The usual, I suppose. According to my brother, Rob, my mother's acting weird again, and Jessica's a bit upset because Ryan has to go away to work.'

He gave a sympathetic nod. 'It's not the best timing, is it? How far advanced is her pregnancy?' He hazarded a guess. 'Third trimester?'

She nodded, smiling. 'Thirty-seven weeks or thereabouts. The baby could decide to put in an appearance any time now.'

His mouth made a flat line. 'Not a great time for her to be on her own, then?'

'No.' Sophie frowned. 'Mum and my stepdad are fairly close by for her, though.'

She glanced around as she heard the sound of footsteps approaching. 'Your table's over here, sir,' the waitress was saying, showing Lord Branscombe to a table set in a quiet corner by the wrought-iron balustrade. As he followed her, Lord Branscombe was walking slowly, each step measured and cautious. He straightened, looking towards the table. A bright spray of scarlet surfinia spilled over from a tall cream-coloured planter nearby and beyond the rail there was a mass of green shrubbery, providing a modicum of privacy from some of the other diners.

James Branscombe acknowledged the waitress briefly, but came to a halt halfway across the terrace. He seemed to be struggling for breath, a hand clutched to his chest, and the waitress watched him worriedly.

'Are you all right?' she asked. 'I didn't think—The steps up to the terrace are quite steep... Perhaps I should have taken it more slowly...'

'Please, don't fuss,' he said in a gruff voice. 'Just bring me a whisky, will you?'

'Of course. Right away.' His command had been peremptory but, even so, the girl escorted Lord Branscombe to his table and made sure he was seated before she hurried away to get his drink.

Around them, Sophie noticed the hubbub of

conversation had died down. People cast surrep-
titious glances towards the occupant of the table
in the corner and then began to speak in hushed
voices. Lord Branscombe, for his part, ignored
them all, lost in a world of his own. In his early
sixties, he looked older, his hair greying, his face
taut and a deep furrow etched into his brow.

'Perhaps he shouldn't be out and about,' Jake
murmured, echoing what everyone must surely
be thinking. 'He doesn't look well.'

'No, he doesn't,' Sophie said, a touch of bitter-
ness threading her words. 'But when did that ever
stop him?'

'True.' He sent her a quick worried look. 'I'm
sorry. Of course, you know that to your cost.'

'It's probably the reason Nate's back at the
Manor House,' she said, ignoring his last state-
ment. She wished she'd never said anything. After
all, what was the point in raking up past history?
'He'll be worried about his father.'

'Hmm…about the estate too, I imagine.' Jake
frowned. 'You must have heard the rumours going
around?'

'About Lord Branscombe's business venture overseas?'

He nodded.

'Yes, I've heard them.' She winced. 'According to what I've read in the national papers, he's lost an awful lot of money.'

'Nate won't like that—the fact that the press have got hold of the story, I mean.'

'No, he won't.' Nate already hated the press after the coverage his father had received a couple of years ago when he was taken ill at the controls of a light aircraft. This new story would have stirred his dislike of them all over again. 'What makes it worse is that he didn't want his father to have anything to do with the so-called development out there in the first place, but Lord Branscombe wouldn't listen.'

'Oh?' Jake raised a brow. 'How do you know that?'

'I heard Nate and his father having a heated discussion one day when I was out walking the dog. Lord Branscombe wouldn't listen to reason... but then, he never has.' And it was James Branscombe's refusal to take heed of what people said that had left her father in the state he was now. Her lower lip began to quiver slightly and she caught it between her teeth to still the movement.

Jake laid his hand over hers, clasping her fingers in a comforting gesture. 'This must be really difficult for you, after what happened to your father.'

'It is.' She closed her eyes fleetingly. Her father had been a passenger in the single-engine plane that crashed nearly two years ago. James Branscombe had taken the controls against all advice and that decision had left her father with life-changing injuries. He'd suffered a broken back, shoulder and ankle, whereas Lord Branscombe had come out of it relatively unscathed.

Even now she had trouble coming to terms with what had happened.

Jake was concerned. 'You must be upset at the thought of Nate coming back. You and he had something going for a while, didn't you? Until the accident put an end to it.'

'Maybe I had feelings for him, years ago, when I was a teenager, and then later it all came to the fore again just before my father's accident…but we wouldn't have made it work. I realise that, now. We were both studying in different parts of the country for a long while, so I didn't see him very often…and, anyway, Nate could never commit to a relationship. Things went badly wrong for us after what happened to my father. I think Nate only stayed around long enough to make sure his father was okay. He's been back a few times since then, but I've kept out of his way.' She braced her shoulders. 'Do you mind if we don't talk about it?'

Right now she couldn't cope with having it all dredged up again. She steeled herself to put on an appearance of calm and she and Jake talked quietly for a while.

A few minutes later, though, her outward composure was all but shattered once more. She looked up and saw a man striding confidently across the terrace, heading towards the corner table.

'Nate?' The word crossed her lips in a whisper of disbelief and Jake gently squeezed her hand in support. It was a shock, seeing Nate standing just a short distance away from her. When she'd seen him, soon after the crash, she'd been upset, out of her mind with worry, and they'd argued furiously over his father's actions. But when he went away, in her mind, in her soul, she'd still yearned for him.

Nate hadn't seen her yet as he stopped briefly to speak to one or two people along the way. Her mind skittered this way and that, trying to find some means of escape, but of course it was hopeless from the start.

He saw her and his eyes widened in recognition. For a moment or two he seemed stunned. Then he started towards her, a long, lean figure of a man, his stride rangy and confident, the muscles in his arms hinting at a body that was perfectly honed beneath the designer T-shirt and casual trousers he was wearing.

The breath caught in her throat. She couldn't think straight any more. All she could do was drink in his image—the broad shoulders, the sculpted cheekbones and the black, slightly over-

long, unruly hair that kinked in a roguish kind
of way.

'Sophie.' His voice was deep and warm, a hint
of satisfaction there, as though he was more than
pleased to see her. He stopped by her table and
looked at her, his brooding green gaze all-en-
compassing, tracing the slope of her cheekbones
and the soft curve of her mouth and lingering on
the golden corkscrew curls that tumbled over her
shoulders. 'It's good to see you again. You look
wonderful.'

Unsettled by that penetrating scrutiny, she lowered her gaze. She didn't know how to react to
him after all this time. She was distracted by a
whole host of unfamiliar feelings that were cours-
ing through her.

His glance trailed downwards, taking in the way
Jake's hand covered hers. Then he lifted his head,
making a faint, almost imperceptible nod. 'Jake.'
He gave him a narrowed look and Jake must have
begun to feel uncomfortable because he straightened, slowly releasing Sophie's hand.

'Hi there, Nate. We haven't seen you in a while,' he said.

'I've been busy, working away for the last few months.' Nate's gaze swept over Sophie once more, meshing with hers in a simmering, wordless exchange.

Images flashed through her mind, visions of times past when they'd walked together through the woods on the estate, when her feelings for him were growing with each day that passed. Nate had held her hand, that last day before she went away to Medical School, and led her into a sunlit copse. She'd been eighteen then, troubled about going away and perhaps not seeing him again. She recalled how the silver birch trees had lifted their branches to the clear blue sky and he'd gently eased her back against the smooth white bark. He'd lowered his head towards her and his kiss had been warm and tender, as soft as the breeze on a hot summer's day.

Even now, thinking about it, she could feel his body next to hers, remember how it had been to be wrapped in his arms, to have her flesh turn to flame as his lips nuzzled the curve of her neck.

Jake's voice broke the spell. 'I'd heard something about you being in the States for a while,' he said. 'You've been doing well for yourself, or so they say.'

'I guess so.' Nate turned his attention to Sophie once more. 'I was hoping we might run into one another.'

'I suppose it was inevitable.' Sophie pulled in a deep breath to steady herself. 'You're back here for your father, I imagine?' She looked up at Nate, amazed to find that her voice worked, with barely a trace of nervousness showing through.

'I am. He's not been doing so well these last few weeks, though he would never admit it.' He frowned, glancing to where his father was sitting alone at the table. 'I should go and join him.' There was a hint of reluctance about his mouth as he spoke. 'But I'd like to see you again, find out how you've been doing. I've tried to keep up with how things were going for you and your father, through Charlotte, mostly.' He looked at her intently. 'Perhaps we could talk later?'

She gave a non-committal movement of her head. Charlotte was the housekeeper at the Manor House and she might have expected her to let Nate know what was happening in the village. As to talking with him, surely it would be best, from her viewpoint, to steer very clear of both Branscombes, but especially Nate? Already she was conscious of a knot forming in her stomach and a fluttery feeling growing in her chest. In every way he was dangerous to her peace of mind. Her alarm system was on full alert.

Nate must have taken her gesture for agreement. He nodded once more to both of them and then left, walking over to the table at the corner of the terrace. As Nate went to sit opposite his father, Sophie saw that another man had come to join them—a man she recognised as Lord Branscombe's Estate Manager...his most recent Estate Manager. Her father had done the job for a good many years before him. She sucked in a sharp breath.

Jake's gaze followed them. 'I wonder what will happen to the estate if Lord Branscombe really has lost most of his money overseas. That's what the newspaper articles are saying...that he's gambled his son and heir's inheritance on a doomed investment and lost.'

'I think there's a lot more to worry about than Nate's inheritance. There are more than two dozen houses on the estate with tenants who will be worried about what's going to happen to their homes.'

Jake's expression was sombre. 'And your father's one of them. It's understandable if you, of all people, feel angry about the way Lord Branscombe's behaved.'

'Maybe.' She frowned. 'But, like I said, I think I'd prefer not to talk about that right now.'

'Of course. But at least it sounds as though Lord Branscombe's finally getting his comeuppance.'

She didn't answer. The waitress came and refilled Sophie's coffee cup, glancing surreptitiously over to where Nate was sitting. Absently, she went to pour a refill for Jake.

'None for me, thanks,' he said, covering his cup with his hand.

'Oh, okay.' Still casting quick looks in Nate's direction, the girl slowly walked away.

Jake made a wry smile. 'He's lost none of his charm, has he?' he murmured, glancing at Sophie. 'He still has that charisma that had all the girls hankering after him.' There was a hint of envy in his voice.

'Mm hmm.' She was hardly immune to it herself—no matter how much she'd told herself in the intervening years that Nate didn't have any power over her feelings, it had taken only a few seconds in his company for him to prove her profoundly wrong. 'I suppose so.'

They chatted for a while, about Jake's work and her job as a children's doctor, until, reluctantly, he glanced once more at his watch. 'I should go,' he said. 'Do you want me to see you back to your car?'

She shook her head. 'No, that's all right. I still have to finish off this coffee. You go ahead. I'll leave in a minute or so.'

'Okay.' He stood up, leaning over to give her a quick, affectionate kiss on the cheek. 'I'll see to the bill on my way out.'

'Thanks.' Sophie watched him leave and then slowly sipped her coffee. It was hot, a new brew fresh from the pot, so she had to take her time. Lord Branscombe, she noticed, glancing idly towards his table, was picking at a plate of food with hardly any appetite, while his Estate Manager was tucking in to a steak and all the trimmings. Nate wasn't eating. The three men seemed to be having an avid discussion about something—the way forward, she supposed.

A short time later she pushed her cup away and picked up her handbag, getting ready to leave.

'You're going already?' Nate must have been watching her because he suddenly appeared at her side, his hand coming to support her elbow as she stood up. 'I didn't want you to leave without my having the chance to talk to you again. Perhaps I could walk with you?'

'I... Yes...I mean...' She was flustered, startled by the way he'd homed in on her, and she stayed

silent as he accompanied her down the stairs. By
the time they reached the lounge area of the restaurant, though, she had managed to recover her
equilibrium enough to say, 'Won't your father be
expecting you to keep him company?'

'I'm sure he'll be fine without me for a while.
Besides, I've said all I need to say to him for now.
He knows my opinion. I've no doubt he and Mau-
rice will be battling things out for another hour
or so yet.'

They walked out of the white-painted building
and stood by the railings on the cliff path, looking out over the rugged crags to the beach below.
'I suppose I shouldn't have been surprised to see
you with Jake,' Nate said. 'You were always good
friends…but I saw that he kissed you. Are you
and he a couple now?' He was studying her intently. 'Are things serious between you?'

She blinked at the suddenness of the question.
She'd forgotten how direct he could be. 'Oh, we
met up again fairly recently,' she answered cautiously. 'I think he's fond of me but, really, we're
just friends.' She suspected Jake would like to

take things further, but after a couple of ill-fated relationships over the last few years, she wasn't about to step into another one in a hurry. Perhaps *she* was the problem. She'd seen what had happened with her parents' marriage and she wasn't ready to put her trust in anyone any time soon.

'I see.' He studied her closely as though gauging her response. He didn't seem to believe the 'just friends' scenario. 'I've always cared for you, Sophie. You know that, don't you? It was hard for me to see you hurting so much after what happened to your father. I felt perhaps you blamed me in some way—perhaps you thought I should have tried to stop my father from flying—'

'You must have known he had angina.' She stared at him, and the pain must have been clear in her eyes. 'Surely there was something you could have done?'

His gaze travelled over her, searing her with its intensity. 'You know what he's like. He never admits to weakness. And I was working at a hospital in Cornwall at the time.' His mouth flattened. 'Sophie, I never wanted there to be this rift between us. You didn't seem to want me around but I always hoped—'

She stopped him before he could say any more. 'No—let's not go there,' she said quickly, anxious to ward off complications. He'd gone away to work abroad, leaving her to pick up the pieces. Perhaps, like he'd said, it was hard for him to see her pain, to witness the heartache his father had caused. 'A lot's happened in the last few years. I'm sure we're very different people now—leastways, I know I am. These past two years have changed me.' She braced her shoulders. 'So what's happening with you? Is there someone in your life these days?'

He pulled a face and shrugged. 'You know me,' he said. 'Can't settle—too much going on all the while.'

'Hmm. And it's going to take time, isn't it, to find the right woman…the one with the class and breeding to take her place at Branscombe Manor?' She said it with a smile, with the wry knowledge that he would most likely exhaust all possibilities before making his pick.

'Oh, you know me so well, don't you?' he said with a short laugh, reading her mind. 'Or at least you always thought you did.' He sobered, studying her thoughtfully.

'Oh, cryptic now, are we?' She let that one pass and asked seriously, 'So…have you come back to sort out the estate?'

He raised a dark brow. 'Can you imagine my father letting me do that? He's never listened to any ideas that don't go along with his way of thinking, from me or anyone. That's why we argued and it's another reason why I left. He's always been a stubborn man, determined to do things his own way.'

'Yes, but you can be a bit like that sometimes,' she said, challenging him. 'Isn't there a bit of *like father, like son*? After all, you decided on medicine as a career and went your own way, even though you knew your father was set against it.'

'True,' he conceded, 'but I felt very strongly about becoming a doctor. I'm lucky, far more fortunate than a lot of people—I was able to dip into my trust-fund money to get me through university because he wouldn't support me in my choice. He wanted me to go in a completely different direction and learn everything there was about Estate Management so that I could take over one day, but I couldn't do what he asked. We settled the argument eventually, but it was always a sore point with him.'

'Some people around here think you don't care about the estate, or the village.'

'Is that what you believe?' He shot her a lancing green stare.

'I think I know you better than that…but I'd like to hear your side of things.'

He made a grimace. 'It's not true that I don't care. Of course I care. It's my heritage. The Manor has been in our family for generations and I want to keep it that way. I would have been fine with taking on the estate when the time came. I would have done whatever was needed, with the help of managers and estate workers, but my father wouldn't tolerate any of my ideas. Whenever I suggested changes that I felt would be for the better, he said things were all right as they were. He made things impossible for me. I wasn't prepared to be just a figurehead, keeping things ticking along in the same old way.'

She nodded, acknowledging the truth of that. Her father had often hinted at how difficult it was to work with Lord Branscombe. 'How are you getting along with him now that you're back?'

He shrugged. 'We still don't see eye to eye, but we get on fine. When I heard that his angina was worsening I had to come back, to make sure he's all right. I didn't see that I had any choice. My father can be difficult, but he's all I have and I'm his only son, so, despite our differences, we have a strong bond. We've come through a lot together over the years and we've learned to understand one another.'

'And how is he, really? He hasn't been looking too good lately.'

'Do you care?' His gaze narrowed on her, a muscle in his jaw flexing. 'After what happened to your father, do you actually care what happens to him?'

She winced as his shot struck home. 'If I'm hon-

est, I'd like to be able to say…no, I don't care…
but I'm a human being and I'm a doctor, so it's
probably inbuilt in me to show concern for anyone who's suffering. I still blame him for what
happened to my father, but I can't do anything to
change the past, can I? Somehow, I have to try to
accept it and move on.'

He sighed. 'I'm sorry, Sophie. I'd give anything
for it not to have happened.' He reached for her,
his hand lightly smoothing over the bare skin of
her arm. His touch disarmed her, sending a trail
of fire to course through her body and under-
mine all her carefully shored-up defences. Against
all common sense she found herself desperately
wanting more.

She couldn't think clearly while he was touching her, holding her this way. She looked at him,
absorbing his strong features, the proud way he
tilted his head, and wished more than ever that
things could be different between them. But it
could never be. Not when his father was responsible for the accident that caused her father's terrible injuries.

'I know you're sorry…but it's too late for regrets now, isn't it? If you'd known about his angina earlier, you might have stopped him from taking off that day. But you didn't.' The words came out on a breathless whisper as she gently eased herself away from him. A look of anguish briefly crossed his face and she said quietly, 'I suppose Charlotte has been making sure you knew how your father was getting along?'

'Yes—if it had been left to him I would never have known how serious his condition had turned out to be. He's far too stubborn for that. But Charlotte has been keeping me up to date, especially after the newspaper stories came out about the investments failing and he took a turn for the worse. We all thought his angina was under control, but his condition has deteriorated and it's become unstable of late.'

She nodded. 'Charlotte's always been more than just a housekeeper to you, hasn't she—from when you were little?'

He smiled. 'That's right. She's looked out for me ever since I was nine years old—from when my mother died. She was always there for me when I needed her. She always seemed to know what was going on in my head, the things that frustrated me or made me happy. Truthfully, she's been like a second mother to me. I'll always want to keep her close.'

She smiled. 'I know. I've always liked Charlotte.' She gazed up at him. From a very young age he'd had a number of pseudo-stepmothers foisted on him as his father brought home a succession of girlfriends, but Charlotte had stayed through it all, his salvation, the one fixed point in his young life that never wavered.

It had been hard for him back then. Going round and about the village with him and their friends as they grew up, Sophie had seen the effect the loss of his mother had on him. Perhaps seeing his vulnerability was what had drawn her to him in the first place. His father hadn't known how to deal with such a young, bewildered and frustrated boy and simply lost himself in keeping up with his contacts in the business world, in the City. Gradually, Nate had built a shell around himself.

No one was going to penetrate his armour…no one except Sophie. Her parents had been going through a difficult time in their marriage and she and Nate had been like kindred souls.

Nate shot her a quick glance. 'She told me she hasn't seen your father in a while. Usually she sees him around the village, at the post office or the grocery store at least once a week, but lately she's missed him.' His voice deepened with concern. 'How is he? Is he still able to get about in the wheelchair?'

'Yes—he's not been out and about lately because he's getting over a nasty chest infection but he manages very well, all things considered.'

'I heard he was having specialist treatment?'

'Yes, that's right. He was in hospital for a long time, as you know, and we were afraid he might never walk again—but thankfully he's making progress. His spinal cord wasn't cut right through, but it has taken a long time to heal, along with the broken bones—he still has physiotherapy several times a week. It's a struggle for him, but he's not one to give up. He generally tries to take things one day at a time. We're hoping that he'll be able to walk with a frame before too long.'

'I'm so sorry, Sophie. If there's anything I can do—' He tried to reach for her but she took a step backwards. It was far too unsettling to have him touch her. Frowning, he let his arms fall to his sides.

'It's all right; I know you would do anything you can to help.'

'My father said he tried to make amends but your father won't talk to him—all their communication is being carried out through lawyers.'

'That's right.' She shot him a quick glance. 'Do you blame him?'

'I suppose not…but nothing's ever going to be achieved by not talking to one another.'

Her back stiffened. 'The accident changed everything. He should never have gone up in that plane with your father—Lord Branscombe seemed unwell from the first but he insisted he was perfectly fit and able to fly. We'd no idea he was suffering from a heart condition. He should have been stopped. It wasn't even as though the journey was important. He just wanted to check out the site of a new golf course he was planning.' She wrapped her arms around herself in a protective gesture. 'It was totally Lord Branscombe's fault, but afterwards he replaced my father as Estate Manager and didn't even offer him a desk job overseeing things.'

Nate frowned. 'My father said he and the lawyers were talking about compensation.'

She gave a short humourless laugh. 'Compensation? What compensation? Your father had been having angina attacks for some time without telling the authorities. He knew it would affect his pilot licence if he said anything—and when the insurance company found out about that they wouldn't pay out. My father lost everything—his job, his house. He had to sell up and go into rented property.'

'I know—he's in one of the houses on the estate.' Nate's eyes darkened. 'It was me who made sure he had somewhere to go… As for the rest, my father said everything was being dealt with. I'm sorry if that wasn't the case…I've been working away quite a bit in the States, so I couldn't oversee things for myself. I wanted to, but…you didn't seem to want me around and then this job came up…I thought, perhaps, you would find it easier if I wasn't around…'

She turned her back to the sea and leaned against the railing, facing him. She wouldn't be drawn into that conversation again, not now. It was too difficult. 'Will you be going back there?'

'No, this last stint was just a six-months contract in the paediatric intensive care unit in Boston. I have a job lined up here in Devon, so I'll be able to keep an eye on things from now on. It's what I've been working towards. This business with my father just moved things forward a bit.' His gaze moved over her, gliding over her slender curves, outlined by the simple sheath dress she was wearing. 'Better still,' he said in a roughened voice, 'it means I'll be able to see more of you. Perhaps you and I could start over…?'

Her heartbeat quickened and her cheeks flushed with heat. 'Oh, I wouldn't be too sure about that,' she countered in a low voice, her throat suddenly constricted. If Nate thought he could erase the last two years and swoop back into her life, he had another think coming.

'Are you sure about that?' He was looking at her in that devilish way that had her nervous system on red alert and he was moving closer, the glint in his green eyes full of promise…

It was a promise that never came to fruition. Shouts came from above them, shocking her system and acting like a dash of cold water to propel them away from one another.

'Help, someone…come quickly—we need help here! Is Nate Branscombe still around? Is that his car in the car park?'

Startled, Sophie looked up to where the sound came from, up on the restaurant's terrace. She saw people getting to their feet, rushing towards the corner table, barely visible from this angle.

A man came to lean over the balustrade, looking down at them, waving his arms urgently. 'Nate, will you come up? It's your father. He's collapsed.'

'Call for an ambulance,' Nate shouted back. He was already taking the steps, racing to get to his father, but instead of following him Sophie hurried towards the car park. Her medical bag was in the boot of her car. Her instincts told her they might need it.

When she reached the corner table a few minutes later, she could see that James Branscombe was sitting propped up against the balustrade. His skin looked clammy, ashen as he groaned in pain. Sophie guessed he was having a bad angina attack, which meant his heart wasn't receiving enough oxygen and had to work harder to get what it needed.

Nate had loosened his father's shirt collar and was kneeling by him, talking to him quietly and trying to reassure him. 'Is your nitro spray in your pocket?' he asked, but James Branscombe was barely able to speak. Nate searched through his pockets until he found what he was looking for and then quickly sprayed the liquid under his father's tongue. The medication would dilate the blood vessels, allowing blood to flow more easily and thereby lessening the heart's workload.

Nate glanced at Sophie as she came to kneel

down beside him. His expression was grim; his fear for his father was etched on his face. He seemed relieved to see that Sophie was by his side, though. 'You have your medical bag?' he said. 'That's good. Do you have aspirin in there?'

'I do—they're chewable ones, or he can dissolve them on his tongue.' She opened the case and handed him the tablets. They would thin the blood and hopefully would prevent blood clots from closing up the arteries.

After a few minutes, though, it was clear that Lord Branscombe was still in a lot of pain. His features were grey, his lips taking on a bluish colour, and beads of cold sweat had broken out on his brow. Sophie guessed this was more than a bad angina attack. She was worried for Nate; this must be something he'd dreaded, the real reason he'd come home.

'Morphine?' Nate asked, and she nodded.

'Yes, I have it. I'll prepare a syringe.'

'Thanks.' He administered the pain medication and soon afterwards wrapped a blood pressure cuff around his father's arm. 'He's becoming hy-

potensive,' he said, frowning. 'I'll put in an intravenous line—as soon as the paramedics get here
we can put him on a saline drip to stabilise his
blood pressure.'

They didn't have to wait too long. The ambulance arrived shortly, siren blaring, and the two
paramedics hurried on to the terrace. They nodded to Sophie, recognising her from her work at
the hospital.

Nate swiftly introduced himself and said, 'I
think my father's having a heart attack. We need
to get an ECG reading and send it to the Emergency department.'

'Okay. We'll make sure they're kept informed.'

'Thank you.'

One of the paramedics set up the portable ECG
machine, whilst the other man began to give the
patient oxygen through a mask. Nate helped them
to lift his father on to a stretcher, and then together they carried him down to the waiting ambulance.

'His blood pressure's dropping.' The paramedic
sounded the alarm and Nate reacted swiftly, set-

ting up a saline drip and giving his father drugs to support his heart's action. Sophie stood by as the three men worked on Lord Branscombe.

'He's gone into V-fib. Stand clear.' Nate called out a warning as his father's heart rhythm went awry and the defibrillator readied itself to give a shock to the heart. He checked his father's vital signs. 'And again, stand clear.'

Her heart went out to him as he exhausted every effort to save his father's life. She saw the worry etched on his face and suddenly wanted to put her arms around him and comfort him, but of course she couldn't do anything of the sort.

'All right,' he said eventually. 'He's stable for now. I'll go with him to the hospital.'

The paramedic nodded. 'Okay, we're ready to go. The emergency team's alerted and waiting for him.'

'That's good.' Nate turned to Sophie, who was waiting by the ambulance doors. 'I want to thank you for all your help,' he said softly. He reached out and gently cupped her arms with his long fingers. 'I owe you. I'll make it up to you, Sophie, I promise.'

She shook her head, making her soft curls quiver and dance. 'There's no need for you to do that. I was glad to help.' No matter what bad feelings she might harbour about James Branscombe, she couldn't have stood by and done nothing to save him. Working alongside Nate, though, had been another matter entirely. She hadn't been prepared for that and the effect it had on her at all.

The paramedic closed the doors of the ambulance and climbed into the driver's seat. Sophie stood by the roadside and watched the vehicle pull away and it was as though the world was sliding from under her feet. She reached out to rest a hand on a nearby drystone wall.

Nate had been back for only five minutes and already she felt as though she'd been hit by an electric storm. How on earth was she going to cope, knowing he meant to stay around and once more make his home at Branscombe Manor?

CHAPTER TWO

'COME ON IN, then, Charlie.' Sophie let herself into her father's kitchen and then stood to one side to let the excited yellow Labrador follow her. He was carrying his lead in his mouth as usual—she always let him walk home the last few yards untethered. She went over to the sink and filled the dog bowl with fresh cold water. 'Okay, I'll swap you—you give me the lead and I'll let you have the water.' It was a ritual they followed every time they went out.

Charlie obligingly dropped the loop handle and she unclipped the lead from his collar and put it away. He drank thirstily and then dropped to the floor, panting heavily and watching her as she washed her hands and then filled the kettle and switched it on.

She gazed out of the window at the neat lawn

and the garden with its bright flower borders. There were scarlet surfinias in tubs that reminded her of that day at the restaurant when she'd met up with Nate. It had been almost two weeks ago and she hadn't seen anything more of him since then but she guessed he was probably spending a lot of his time visiting his father in the Coronary Care Unit.

'He looks suitably worn out.' Her father wheeled himself into the kitchen, breaking into her thoughts and smiling as he looked over at the dog. 'Just as well, if the physio's coming here later on. Charlie can be a bit too exuberant at times.'

Sophie smiled with him and pushed a cup of tea across the table towards him. 'He's not slowing down at all, is he? You'd have thought at eight years old there would have been a few signs of maturity by now, wouldn't you?'

'You would.'

Her father had bought Charlie as a pup, a couple of years after his marriage to her mother had broken down. He'd taken him with him everywhere, even to his work on the estate, and they'd roamed the woods and fields together, man and dog.

'How's the work going with the physio?' she asked now, as she slid bread into the toaster. Every morning before work, she came over to the house to have breakfast with her father.

'We're getting there, I reckon.' He paused, thinking about it. 'When she came yesterday I stood for a while with the frame, and I even managed to take a couple of steps.'

'You did?' He looked deservedly pleased with himself and Sophie stopped what she was doing and rushed over to him. 'Oh, that's wonderful.' She hugged him fiercely. 'I'm thrilled to bits for you. That's amazing.'

'Yes, it's definitely a step forward...' He chuckled at his own joke and she laughed with him. 'Seriously, with all the treatment I've been having at the hospital, and now these sessions at home with the physio, I feel as though I'm making progress. It's been a long job, but I'm getting there at last.'

They ate cereals and toast and chatted for a while, but Sophie soon realised her father had something else on his mind. 'I've been hearing rumours,' he said, 'about Branscombe losing all his money and the estate houses being put on the market. Do you know anything about that?'

'Not really.' She frowned. 'I don't suppose we'll know anything more until Lord Branscombe is out of hospital. Nate's looking after things in the meantime, but—'

'You've seen him again?' Martin Trent's voice was sharp, his whole manner on the alert all at once.

'No...no, not since I saw him that day at the Seafarer when his father was taken ill.' Sophie hastily tried to calm him. It was true. She hadn't *seen* him. She wasn't going to tell him that she'd phoned the Manor House the next day to find out how Lord Branscombe was faring. After all, it had been an innocent enquiry—she'd expected to talk to Charlotte, and it had been a shock to have Nate answer the phone.

'I haven't seen him,' she said again, calmly, concerned that her father was still looking tense, his fingers gripping tightly on the arms of his wheelchair, 'so I assume he's busy visiting his father and talking to the Estate Manager to see how they can keep things jogging along.'

'Hmmph.' He slumped back in his seat. 'I don't want either of us to have anything more to do with that family. James is an arrogant, self-centred womaniser and his son is likely no better.'

'We don't know that Nate is like that,' she said in a reasonable tone. 'He hasn't been around here for any length of time these past few years, has he, so how can we judge him?'

'He can't escape heredity,' her father said flatly. 'It'll be in the genes. That's all you need to know. Besides, he upset you…I know you and he argued but you were broken-hearted when he went away.'

'It was a bad time. You were injured and struggling to come to terms with being disabled and I was confused and lashed out.' Sophie sighed inwardly. She understood her father's dislike of the Branscombes and his hostility towards them. After all, he'd worked for Lord Branscombe for years and had suffered in the end because of it, but it was hard for her to share his animosity towards the son. Her mind drifted back to that last conversation she'd had with Nate.

He'd been more than pleased to talk to her that day when she'd telephoned the Manor House. Despite his troubles, his voice was warm and welcoming, sending little thrills to run along her spine. Just hearing him had made her feel that he was close by, almost as though he was in the room with her. She'd been concerned for him, though, wondering how he was bearing up, and tried to keep her mind on the business in hand.

'They're assessing my father in the Coronary Care Unit,' he'd said when she asked about Lord Branscombe. 'I think they're planning on removing the blood clot and putting a stent in one of his arteries. It's looking as though he'll be in hospital for some time.'

They'd talked for a while and he said, 'I'm sorry things turned out the way they did—both for my father and for selfish reasons… It was good seeing you again, Sophie. I'm sorry our get-together came to such an abrupt end.'

'Yes…though I wasn't expecting you to turn up that day or I—' She broke off.

'Or you'd have gone out of your way to avoid me.' She could hear the wry inflection in his voice and she flinched, knowing what he said was the truth.

Seeing him again had stirred up all sorts of feelings inside her that she'd thought were long since forgotten…or at least pushed to one side. But she didn't want to go there again—to start up something that would only end in distress.

Suddenly uncomfortable, she sought for a way to bring the conversation to an end. 'I'm sure your father's in good hands, Nate. He'll be glad to have you by his side as he recovers.'

'Yes, he seems calmer, knowing I'm here for him.'

'That's good.' She hesitated, cautious about getting more deeply involved with him, and then said, 'I should go. Maybe I'll see you around.'

'Sophie, couldn't we—?' Nate started to speak but she quickly cut the call before she could change her mind.

'Bye.' She had no idea what he must have made of her rush to get away, but he already knew she was trying to keep her distance from him.

'Anyway,' her father was saying, 'it looks as though the tenancies could be at risk if what the papers say is true.' His brow was furrowed with anxiety. 'I've grown used to living here since the crash—I have wheelchair access, handrails... I don't want to have to move...to have to go through the upheaval all over again...'

'It probably won't come to that,' she said, trying to soothe him. 'I suppose we're all in much the same boat—my place is rented too. But, as far as I know, the press stories are just speculation. It's too soon yet for anything to have been decided.'

'Yes, I suppose you're right.' He glanced at Charlie, snoozing in the corner of the kitchen. 'Thanks for taking him out for me every day. It's good of you and I do appreciate what you do for me—I know how hard you work.'

She smiled at him and stood up to clear away the breakfast dishes. 'I like to keep an eye on you. I was worried when you had that chest infection, but you look so much better now.' She finished tidying up and then glanced at her watch. 'I must go,' she said. 'I have a date first thing with those gorgeous little babies in the Neonatal Unit.'

'Ah…that's the bit you like best of all about your job, isn't it? Looking after the tiny infants.'

'It is.' She gave him a quick kiss and a hug, patted a sleepy Charlie on the head and headed out of the door.

She drove to work, following the coast road for a while, uplifted as always by the sight of the wide, sweeping bay and the rugged landscape of cliffs and inlets. After a mile or two she turned inland, driving along a country road until gradually it gave way to suburbia and eventually the local town came into view. She parked the car at the hospital and made her way inside the building.

There was one baby in particular she was eager to see this morning. Alfie had been born prematurely at twenty-seven weeks and had been looked after in Intensive Care for the last couple of months. She'd followed his progress day by day. Now that he was a little stronger and in a better stage of development, Sophie had been able to withdraw his nasogastric feeding tube and she was keen to see how he and his mum were coping with him taking milk from a bottle. They'd had a few attempts at feeding him over the last couple of days, but so far it hadn't been going too well.

'Hi there, Mandy,' Sophie greeted the young woman who was sitting by the baby's cot, holding the infant in her arms. She looked down at the tiny baby, his little fingers clenched, his pink mouth pouting, seeking nourishment. 'Isn't he gorgeous?'

Mandy smiled agreement, though at the moment the baby was squirming, crying intermittently and obviously hungry. The nurse on duty brought a bottle of milk and handed it to Mandy, who gently placed the teat in her baby's mouth.

Alfie sucked greedily, gulped, swallowed and forgot to breathe, causing him to choke on the milk, and Mandy looked anxious. 'He keeps doing that,' she said worriedly.

'It's all right, Mandy,' Sophie said softly. 'It's something they have to learn, to remember to breathe while they're feeding. Sometimes they stop breathing for a few seconds because the heart rate is a little slow—as in Alfie's case—but we've added a shot of caffeine to his milk to give him a little boost. There's supplemental iron in there too, because being born prematurely means his iron stores are a bit low.'

'Will he always have this low heart rate?' The young mother was full of concern for her baby.

'No, no. Things will get better as he matures. In the meantime, the caffeine will help. You can relax. He's doing really well.' Sophie lightly stroked the baby's hand. 'Look, he's sucking better already.'

She left the unit a few minutes later, after checking up on a couple of other babies, and then went along to the Children's Unit. An eleven-year-old girl had been admitted a couple of days ago, suffering from septicaemia, and she wanted to see how she was doing.

'Sophie—I was hoping I might catch up with you at some point today.' A familiar deep male voice greeted her and stopped her in her tracks. An odd tingling sensation ran through her.

She'd been lost in thought, but now she looked up to see Nate standing by the nurses' station, tall and incredibly good-looking, dressed in dark trousers that moulded his long legs and a pristine shirt with the sleeves folded back to the elbows.

She stared at him, her blue eyes wide with shock, her heart beginning to thump heavily. 'Nate—what are you doing here?' She was startled to see him standing there, and more than a little alarmed to have her sanctuary invaded. This was one place where she'd always thought she was safe.

'I've started a new job here as a locum consultant,' he explained. 'It's a temporary post for the next few months until they appoint a new person for the job. They tell me I'll be in the running for that too.'

She pulled in a steadying breath. 'I'd no idea you were looking for work over here. I suppose you must be pleased that you found something so soon...and so close to home.' Why did it have to be here, in her department? How on earth was she going to cope, having him around?

'I am; I'm very pleased. The opportunity came up and I decided to go for it. This will give me time to decide what I want to do—and of course it means I'll be on hand to visit my father in the Coronary Care Unit here, which is an advantage.'

'Yes, of course.' She looked at him in concern. 'I hope he's doing all right.'

He nodded. 'They went ahead and put a stent in the artery to prevent another blockage there. He's a lot better than he was.'

'That's good.' Her mind was reeling. It was difficult enough, knowing that Nate was back in the village…but to have him here, working alongside her…that was something she'd not contemplated. How was her father going to react to that news? But she didn't confide any of that to Nate. Instead she did her best to keep things on an even keel. 'I hope you enjoy your time here—I think you'll find it's a very friendly, supportive place to work.'

'I'm sure I will.' His green eyes glinted as he looked at her. 'Knowing that you're here too makes it even better.' His glance moved over her, flicking appreciatively over her curves, outlined by the close-fitting lavender-coloured top and dove-grey pencil-line skirt she was wearing. 'I'm more than glad to know that I'll be working alongside you.'

'I—uh…' She cleared her throat. 'Yes…well…I think I should make a start on seeing my patients. I was just about to do a ward round.'

He inclined his head briefly. 'I'll come with you and try to get acquainted with everyone. I've already met some of the doctors and the nursing staff…like Tracey and Hannah over there…' His mouth made a crooked shape and he gestured towards a couple of the nurses who had been watching him from a distance but who now felt dismayed at being discovered and quickly seemed to find a reason to be going about their work.

She acknowledged their reaction with a faint grimace. Nothing had changed, had it? No doubt the nurses and female doctors had been falling over themselves to get to know him. He seemed to have that effect on women. They simply couldn't get enough of him. And he probably liked things that way.

'Okay. I thought I'd start by looking in on Emma.' She began to walk towards one of the wards, a four-bed bay close to the nursing station.

He seemed to be searching his memory. 'That would be the child with sepsis?'

She looked at him in surprise. 'You've looked through the notes already?'

He nodded. 'I like to know who and what I'm going to be dealing with, if at all possible. There isn't always time but I was in early today, so I was able to take a quick glance at the notes on computer. They only give the bare essentials, of course.'

She had to admire his thoroughness. 'Well, she and her friend apparently gave each other body piercings—they wanted to wear belly bars but Emma's mother wouldn't allow it, so they did it in secret. Emma's wound became infected and the little girl was too worried about what her parents would say to tell them what was happening. It was only when she started to feel ill that she finally admitted what she'd done. Her parents brought her to A&E but by then the infection was in her bloodstream.'

He winced. 'You have her on strong antibiotics?'

'We do. We had the results of tests back from the lab—it's an aggressive infection, so we've put her on a specific treatment now. Of course she needs support to compensate for failing internal organs while her body's under attack.'

That was the reason the little girl was on a ventilator to help with her breathing and was receiving vital fluids through an intravenous line. Her parents were sitting by her bedside, taking turns to hold her hand. They were pale and distraught, and Sophie did her best to reassure them.

'Her temperature's down,' she said, glancing at the monitor, 'and her blood oxygen levels are improving, so it looks as though the antibiotics are beginning to have an effect. It will take time, but there's a definite improvement.'

'Thank you.' Emma's mother was still sick with worry. 'I just blame myself. I should have known.'

'I doubt anyone would know if a child made up her mind to keep something to herself,' Nate said, his voice sympathetic. 'It's all the rage to get these piercings, but I expect she'll be wanting to give them a miss for the time being, at least.' He smiled and the woman's mouth curved a fraction.

'Let's hope you're right about that.'

Sophie went on with the ward rounds, conscious all the time of Nate by her side. He talked to the young patients, getting a smile from those who were able and bringing comfort to those who needed it. He was a dream of a children's doctor. It was a role that could have been made especially for him.

'Shall we go and get some lunch in the hospital restaurant?' he suggested a couple of hours later, when she had seen all her patients and finished writing up her notes.

'Yes, I'd like that. I'm starving.'

He grinned. 'I thought you might be. You always burned up energy like a racing engine. From what I've heard, the food's pretty good here.'

'It's not bad at all,' she agreed. 'That's mostly down to Jake's intervention, I think. Soon after he was appointed as a manager, he brought in new caterers and the whole place was reorganised. It's only been up and running for a few weeks. They do hot and cold food and there are sections where you can help yourself and get served quickly.'

He pushed open the door and slipped an arm around her waist as he guided her into the large open-plan area. She felt the warmth of his palm on the curve of her back through the thin material of her top and a sensation of heat spread out along her spine. Try as she might to ignore it, she couldn't get away from the fact that she liked the feel of his hand on her body…so much so that she was almost disappointed when he let go of her and led the way to the service counters.

There were several of them, each offering a variety of food—salads, sandwiches, cold meats, and then there were the hot food counters, serving things like jacket potatoes, chilli con carne and tomato-and-basil quiche.

Nate studied the menu board. 'Looks like today's specials are lasagne or shepherd's pie,' he said.

She pulled herself together and tried to concentrate. 'I think I'll have the lasagne,' she said, and added a rhubarb crumble to her tray. Nate opted for shepherd's pie and runner beans but didn't bother with a dessert. He added a pot of tea and two cups to his tray.

'No pudding… Now I see how you keep that lean and hungry look,' she commented.

'Oh, I prefer savoury food above all else.' His gaze travelled over her. 'But the puddings don't seem to have done you any harm at all. You're as slim as ever—with curves in all the right places.' He smiled as a swift tide of heat swept over her cheeks. 'It must be all the exercise you get, working here and helping your father. Charlotte mentioned to me that you walk the dog and do your father's grocery shopping and so on.'

'I do what I can.' They chose a table by the window and sat down to eat.

'I imagine your father and Jake get on pretty well,' Nate said after a while. 'Jake's easy to get along with, isn't he?'

'I guess so. I mean, he and I get on all right. We always have done.' She frowned. They'd always been friends, a bit like a brother and sister, really. She looked at Nate. 'Actually, he hasn't had all that much to do with my father, up to now. They know one another, of course, from when we were younger, but I haven't had occasion to take him home as yet.'

'Hmm.' His green gaze was thoughtful.

'What's that supposed to mean?'

'I expect Jake wants to move things on... He'll want to be more than just friends.' He studied her intently as though memorising every one of her features. 'Any man would.'

She moistened her lower lip with her tongue. 'I don't know about that. I've been down that road before and I've discovered to my cost that things don't always work out too well.'

He raised a brow. 'Perhaps you've known the wrong people.'

'Perhaps.' The truth was, the only man she'd ever really wanted was Nate, but there had always been so many obstacles in their way that it just felt that maybe it was never meant to be. 'You must know from your father's experience that it isn't easy to find the right partner in life,' she said. 'My own mother and father couldn't make a go of it.'

'I think the truth is my father never really got over losing my mother,' he admitted. 'He was something of a lost soul after that. But, as to your situation, it always struck me—as a child growing up—that your father did his best. He wanted the relationship to work.'

'I'm sure he did.' She pulled a face. 'But, well, you know my mother... She could be...flaky, I suppose you'd call it. She was unreliable and her behaviour was odd sometimes. It made her difficult to live with, but of course we didn't know then that she was suffering from bipolar disorder.'

He slid his fork into his shepherd's pie. 'It must have been difficult for you when the marriage broke up and she took you and your brother and sister away to live in Somerset.'

'Yes, it was. It was hard leaving my father, and everything we'd ever known back here.' She frowned, thinking about it. 'Though it wasn't so bad for me because I was getting ready to go to Medical School. I was more worried about leaving Rob and Jessica behind at that time. They were still very young—nine and eleven by the time Mum remarried. It broke my heart to leave them.' Her mouth flattened. 'I still worry about them after all this time—eight years later.'

'But they come to stay with you quite often, don't they? Charlotte told me a long while ago that they're back here whenever they have the chance.'

'That's true. Jessica's married now, though, so I don't know if she'll be over here quite as much.'

His eyes lit up with interest. 'I heard about that—and that she's pregnant. Is she okay? Is it all going well?'

She paused for a moment to savour her lasagne. 'Yes, she's fine. Money's a bit tight—but she and Ryan managed to buy a small terraced house in an old part of town. They're young and they were impulsive, I suppose, in a hurry to be together. Only now Ryan's taken a job which means he has to work away for several days at a time. I'm just hoping they won't have too much of a struggle financially, with a baby on the way.'

He shrugged lightly. 'Young people are resilient. If the love's there I'm sure nothing much else matters.'

She smiled. 'I think that's what I've always liked about you—your optimism. Yes, I'm sure things will turn out fine, eventually.'

He poured tea for both of them. 'And Rob—how's he getting along? He must be sixteen or seventeen by now...'

'He's just turned seventeen. Rob's a typical teenager—full to bursting with teenage hormones right now.' She made a start on her dessert, enjoying the brief moment of sweetness as she tasted the creamy custard on her tongue. 'I think he worries about Dad.'

'I'm sure he does. The relationship between a father and his son is an important one.' He studied her closely. 'It applies to fathers and daughters too. Your father always looked out for you, didn't he? I had the feeling he didn't want you getting too close to me.'

'He was just trying to protect me. I guess he knew you weren't one to settle. And your family heritage is something you can't get away from—

you lead a vastly different life to most ordinary people and I suppose he felt in your eyes and your father's eyes I would always be the Estate Manager's daughter.'

He shook his head. 'That's not true. I always thought you were special. I was miserable when you left to go to Medical School—I was glad for you that you were doing something you'd always wanted to do, but sad for myself. We were bound to be separated for a great amount of time, studying in different parts of the country.'

She smiled, unconvinced. As a teenager she'd longed for Nate to look at her the way he'd looked at other women, but it was only when her family was uprooted and she was desperately vulnerable that things had changed between the two of them. He'd reached out to her and offered her comfort, a shoulder to cry on.

But it had been too late. She'd made the decision to leave home to go and study medicine. Those last few times they had been together, he had held her in his arms and there had been the occasional stolen kiss, enough to make her long for more. How could she have allowed herself to get more deeply involved with him back then? He was often away, studying to be a doctor, and when he was home she was too conscious of the great divide between them to let it happen.

Perhaps it was true he had missed her for a while. But he must have known that they were miles apart in other ways. Nate's family, unlike hers, was completely orderly, old school, following age-old traditions, their ways of going on passed down from generation to generation. She sighed inwardly. She would never fit in.

Now, he reached for the milk jug and frowned as he caught sight of a newspaper lying abandoned and open on a nearby table. Sophie followed his gaze and scanned the headlines. There was a picture of Branscombe Manor with a larger image of Lord Branscombe in the foreground.

Lord Branscombe puts Village up for Sale! the headline screamed. *Villagers mount protest!*

'Wretched rumour-mongers,' Nate said under his breath. 'Why do they have to go talking to the press?'

Sophie studied the headlines in consternation. 'Is it true? Is the estate up for sale?'

'Nothing's been decided yet,' he answered shortly, his jaw tense. 'But that doesn't stop the rabble-rousers from going tattling to the papers, raking up trouble, does it?'

'People are worried about the future of the village,' she told him with a frown. 'They know what's happened with your father—how he lost a great deal of money—and they want to know what he's planning on doing about it. Surely you can understand that?'

'Of course I do. But my father is too frail to cope with estate matters right now, and stories like this aren't going to help. He made a mistake—he knows that now. He thought he was buying land with a huge potential for development but it failed spectacularly. He's lost millions of pounds. It's a tragedy for everyone concerned and I know how worried people must feel. Right now, though, he's too ill to deal with any of it and he's passed the reins over to me. Somehow or other I have to negotiate a way out of the mess.'

'I'm sorry.' She laid a hand on his arm, sympathising with his predicament and wanting to offer comfort. 'That's a huge burden for you to take on.'

'It's a headache, I grant you.' He squeezed her hand lightly, sending a warm tide of sensation to ripple through her.

As their lunch break drew to a close, they finished their meal and headed back to the Children's Unit. When they reached it, they found everyone on high alert.

'A little boy's being transferred here from Emergency,' Tracey told them. 'I was just about to page you. He'll be here in a few minutes. His name's Josh. He's five years old—apparently, he ran out from behind an ice-cream van yesterday and was hit by a car. He was tossed in the air and hit his head on the ground.'

Sophie sucked in a breath. It was one of the worst things a doctor could hear...and as to the child's parents, they must be in torment. 'How bad is it?'

'His skull's fractured in four places and the CT

scan shows there's a blood clot forming under the bone. The A&E team decided it would be best to keep an eye on things rather than operate. At the moment he's under sedation and on a ventilator.'

'Okay, we'll keep him that way for now. Let's make sure everything's ready for him.' Sophie quickly stifled her emotional response and switched to being professional. 'I'll take a look at him and then go and talk to the parents. Are they being looked after?'

'Hannah's with them at the moment.'

'Good.' Sophie started towards the side ward, getting ready to receive the little boy. She was very much aware of Nate walking along with her, silent and concerned, his expression taut. He'd been rigidly attentive, on the alert the whole time.

'Does this bring back memories for you?' she asked. 'I know you suffered a head injury as a child.'

'Ah...yes, that's very true. I was nine years old and fell from the roof of an old outbuilding near to the Manor House. One of the gardeners found me unconscious on the ground.' He frowned.

'Apparently, my mother was beside herself with worry back then… She stayed with me through two nights, thinking that I might not make it.'

Sophie was concerned for Nate. 'That must have made a lasting impression on you.' It must be one of the last major memories he had of his mother. She'd been killed in a car accident a few months later.

'My accident was the reason I wanted to study medicine. I was so impressed, even at that young age, by the way the doctors and nurses looked after me. I was convinced I had to be able to save lives the same way they saved mine. But my mother's death coming so soon afterwards—the car accident that killed her—was horrendous. It was such a shock. It had a tremendous impact on me and it's something I've struggled to come to terms with over the years…in order to carry on.'

She nodded, understanding. Sophie was almost four years younger than Nate, but even back then, as a little girl, she'd been aware of Nate's unhappiness, the way he'd withdrawn into himself. Now, as an adult, she could still feel terrible sadness for that vulnerable little boy.

'I can't imagine how any child could handle something like that.'

He made a brief faint smile. 'As I recall, you were very gentle and caring with me over the next few years. You talked to me and tried to bring me out of myself. I appreciate that, even now.'

'I'm glad if I was some help.'

She prepared herself as the injured child was wheeled into the side ward. He was deathly pale, breathing oxygen through a tube that had been inserted in his windpipe, and there were tubes and wires connecting him to equipment and monitors used in the transfer.

Immediately, she did a quick but thorough examination. 'Tracey, will you do fifteen-minute observations, please?—limb movement, pupils, blood pressure, temperature and verbal response and so on. We'll need to monitor intracranial pressure. A small blood clot might resolve on its own, but if the swelling gets worse he'll have to go up

to Theatre to have it removed, so everyone needs
to be looking out for that.'

'I'll see to it.' Tracey started on the first round
of observations, noting the results in the patient's
chart.

Sophie and Nate went to talk to the parents.
They were sitting in the waiting room with Hannah, still very upset, but they were calm enough
to recount the incident.

'I carried him to the ambulance,' his father said.
'He was bleeding from his ear and he was so quiet
and limp in my arms. I was scared. I didn't know
what was going to happen to him.'

Stressed, Josh's mother clasped her fingers together. 'We're still in shock,' she said.

'It's a difficult time for you,' Sophie agreed.
'But I promise you we're doing everything we
can to make sure he's comfortable.'

'Is he…is he going to be brain damaged?' The
father voiced what both parents must be thinking.

'I wish I could give you definitive answers,' Sophie said, 'but it isn't possible just now. The healing process takes time but he's young, and young

people have remarkable powers of recovery. We have to be patient and wait and let nature do its work.'

'Dr Trent is very experienced in looking after children with these types of injuries,' Nate said, and Sophie absorbed his comment in surprise. Had he checked up on her qualifications? As the new locum consultant, he would probably have access to staff records. Or maybe the head of the unit had told him all about her. 'We'll let you know about his progress every step of the way,' Nate added. 'You'll be able to sit with him as soon as we have him settled, and we can arrange overnight accommodation in a room close by if one or both of you want to stay with him.'

'Thank you...thank you so much.' Josh's mother wiped away a tear. 'He's so tiny. I can't believe this is happening.'

They talked for a little while longer, and then Sophie and Nate left them in Hannah's care. The nurse would take them along to see their son in a few minutes.

Sophie spent the rest of the afternoon making

sure that Josh's condition remained stable and that her other small charges were being looked after. She scanned lab reports and dictated her notes and then handed over to the doctor who was coming on duty to take her place.

'Are you off home now?' Nate asked, coming after her and watching her retrieve her bag from her locker. 'I expect you have plans for the evening?' He didn't ask her about Jake, but somehow she guessed that was on his mind. He just wouldn't believe that Jake was only a friend...

'Yes, I do, but I have to go and walk Charlie and pick up a few bits from the shops first of all,' she said. 'Aren't you about due to finish your shift too?'

He nodded. 'I'm just going to stay and tidy up a few loose ends before I go. I'll walk with you to your car, though, if that's all right. I could do with a breath of fresh air.'

'That's fine.' They left the hospital together, walking out through the landscaped gardens to the car park beyond. All around them, stretching far into the distance, they could see the beautiful Devon moorland.

Nate took a moment to take it in as they came to stand by her car. 'I love this county,' he said, looking around. 'Whenever I've been away, no matter where I am in the world, I always want to come back here.'

'It's a wonderful place to live,' she agreed. 'I'm certainly glad I came back to the village.' She glanced at Nate, a small line creasing her brow. 'Your ancestral home is here, though, isn't it? How's that going to work out for you? Will the Manor House be safe, with everything that's been happening? You haven't really said anything about how you're going to be affected by all this.'

'I think the house at least should be secure,' he said. 'My father hasn't mentioned any problem with it.'

'But the estate *is* at risk, isn't it?' she persisted. 'I know you don't like to think about it, but the stories in the papers aren't unfounded, are they? Is there any chance that your father will sell up?'

His shoulders moved stiffly. 'He was approached by a would-be buyer—Peninsula Hold-ings—some time ago. He was considering their offer, but then he had his heart attack and everything's been put on hold. He's handed all the business dealings over to me, and I have to make a decision soon, but I still need to make up my mind on the best course of action.'

Sophie frowned. 'I've heard of that company,' she said, suddenly uneasy. 'They're a business conglomerate, aren't they—a company that likes to pull down properties and build hotels in their place?'

'It's true—they're a company generally interested in development, but that doesn't automatically mean they'll want to knock down the cottages on the estate. They might prefer to keep up the tenancies.'

'Really?' She raised a brow at that. 'From what I've heard of their other operations, if they do that they're quite likely to put up the rents—to a level that people can't afford.' Perhaps her father had been right to be worried all along.

'The rents are quite low, and have been for some

time,' Nate said calmly. 'There was some talk of offering people the opportunity to buy their properties rather than rent.'

'My father wouldn't be able to do that.' Sophie shook her head, making her honey-gold curls dance. 'And I'm not sure *I'm* in a position to do that right now either. I'd need to come up with a substantial deposit, and that won't be easy at the moment. I've been doing what I can to help out Jessica—she needed funds when they bought the house—and now I'm helping my father. He's having private physio treatment at the moment, and that doesn't come cheap.'

She frowned. 'Is this development company going to put me out of a home, along with all the rest? Can't you do something to put this right, Nate?' Her blue eyes pleaded with him. 'There are too many people who stand to have their lives turned upside down the way things are at the moment.'

'You don't have any need to worry, Sophie. I won't let anything bad happen to you.'

'No?' She looked at him uncertainly. 'What could you do to make this go away?'

He smiled, a compelling, enticing smile that made her insides quiver with excitement and longing. He slipped his hands around her waist and drew her to him. 'You could always come and live with me at the Manor House. You could have anything you want there. You know I've always wanted to keep you close.'

He lightly caressed the curve of her hips and wrapped his arms around her, drawing her into the shelter of his long, hard body.

Her mind fragmented, her willpower crumbling as she felt the heat emanating from him, felt the powerful muscles of his thighs against her legs. 'I've always wanted you, Sophie,' he whispered.

A pulse throbbed in her temple, and a wave of heat ran through her from head to toe. Her wilful body was saying *yes, yes, please* to the temptation of being with him, locked in his seductive embrace, but the sensible part of her mind was telling her this was madness. What was she thinking of, letting him coax her this way?

'I can't,' she said huskily. 'There's just too much water under the bridge with us, Nate—you know that.' She closed her eyes briefly at the thought. 'Plus, my father would have a stroke.'

'Ah...I wouldn't want that to happen,' Nate murmured. 'But maybe you could bear my offer in mind...for some time in the future, perhaps? There is still something between us; I can feel it...'

She pushed against his chest with the flat of her hand. 'I think that's highly unlikely,' she said.

'Maybe.' A smile played around his mouth. 'But, like you said, I've always been an optimist.'

CHAPTER THREE

'OH, THAT'S GOOD to see. He's feeding much better now, Mandy.' Sophie watched in awe as the tiny infant lay in his mother's arms, suckling hungrily at the bottle of milk formula she was holding. He was wrapped tenderly in a beautiful super-soft Merino wool shawl. Alfie's eyes were wide open, the deepest blue, and he looked up at his mother with perfect trust.

A lump formed in Sophie's throat. She worked with babies and children all the time, but would she ever experience that profound joy of holding her own baby close to her heart? It was a difficult question to answer. The father of her baby would have to be the one and only man for her, the love of her life, because after the disasters that had occurred in her family she didn't want to make the same mistakes they'd made. She wanted a relationship that would stand the test of time…but was that going to be possible?

She closed her eyes briefly. Nate would make a wonderful father… She could see him holding their child in his arms…holding the baby against his bare chest. Unbidden, the image came through in startling clarity, along with a rush of heat that suffused her whole body. Nate was everything she was looking for in a man. He could turn her blood to flame with a single glance and just thinking about him in that way caused a wave of dizziness to engulf her. It could never be…he would never settle, and he wouldn't choose to spend his life with her, the daughter of a man who had worked for his father, would he? How could she contemplate such a thing? She must be out of her mind, even thinking along those lines!

She'd do far better to concentrate on the job in hand, wouldn't she? Chiding herself inwardly, she straightened, finished checking up on her tiny charges and with a new, brisk determination left the Neonatal Unit and went to look in on the rest of her young patients on the Children's

Ward. Thankfully, Nate was nowhere to be seen. She didn't think she could cope with having him around just now.

'He's gone up to the Coronary Care Unit to see his father,' Hannah said when Sophie came across her a little later on. The young nurse frowned, pushing back a stray lock of chestnut-coloured hair. 'They were aiming to get Lord Branscombe out into the rehabilitation garden this morning but he wasn't well enough, apparently. He's been very breathless lately.'

'I'm sorry to hear it.' Sophie frowned. 'Nate must be very worried.'

Hannah nodded. 'He is.' She'd obviously been talking to Nate quite a bit lately. That was the way with him—he got on well with everyone, and the nurses especially had taken to him. Did he return their interest? Sophie wasn't at all happy with the way her thoughts were going—it was quite possible that he would start dating any pretty girl who caught his eye... Wasn't that warning enough that she should steer clear of accepting Nate as anything other than a colleague? Her stomach churned uneasily.

She left Hannah after a minute or so and went to look through the patients' files in the wire trolley by the desk, searching for five-year-old Josh's notes. She and the rest of the team were worried about the little boy's head injury and she wanted to check up on his medication and observation chart. A further CT scan this morning showed there was a very slow bleed beneath the skull bones and the pressure inside his head was rising.

Looking at the little boy this morning had left her feeling worried. Pale and unmoving, his fair hair tousled against the pillow, he'd seemed incredibly vulnerable and her heart turned over at the sight of him. If the medication didn't resolve the problem, she would have to do something fairly soon to prevent a dangerous downturn in his condition.

'Hi there, Sophie.' Jake walked towards her and greeted her, smiling. 'I've been looking for you.'

Surprised to see him, she gave him a quick answering smile. As a hospital manager, he spent most of his time in his office, so she hadn't expected him to venture down here. He wasn't an impulsive man. 'Hello, Jake. Is everything okay?'

'Yes, absolutely fine.' He nodded. 'On the face of it, I'm down here looking for Tracey. I need to ask her to try out a new batch of disposable syringes—but I was hoping to see you. I wanted to tell you that I won't be able to come with you to the village fête on Saturday, after all.'

'Oh, that's a shame.'

'It is.' He looked genuinely downcast. 'I'm sorry—I was really looking forward to spending the day with you, but I have to go and talk to a couple of people I used to work with in Cornwall. They've been trying out a new supplier for things like cannulas and rubber gloves—equipment we use all the time—and they've supposedly made a huge saving in their hospital budget. I'm thinking of using the same supplier here, but I want to know how their trial went before I do that. Saturday's the only day we can all meet up.'

'That's all right. Don't worry about it.' She made an impish grin. 'I'll have Charlie for company. I dare say he'll drag me through all the mud in the playing field before we get to the enclosure where the dog show's taking place.'

'Playing field?' He lifted a brow. 'Oh, you don't know about the change of venue, then?'

'It's not going to be at the school?' She shook her head. 'No, I haven't heard anything...but then, I've been very busy lately, with one thing and another.'

'The school had to cry off—the mobile class-room unit is being delivered ahead of time, so the headmaster asked around to see if any other or-ganisation could offer a field. Nate Branscombe stepped in and told the committee they could use the grounds of the Manor if they wanted. There'll be marquees if the weather turns bad, or the old stable block—it was a better alternative than the village common, by all accounts. Anyway, they're busy putting up notices all over the village.'

'Oh, I see.' That had come as a bit of a shock. She wasn't sure how she felt about spending the day in the grounds of the Manor. She studied Jake thoughtfully. 'How do you know all this—you're not on the committee, are you?'

He shook his head. 'Nate told Hannah and she told Tracey… You know how the grapevine works.'

'Hmm.' Apparently it didn't extend as far as Sophie, but in this instance that might be because they were worried about how she'd feel about going to an event at the home of her father's archenemy. They were probably right to have their doubts…but most likely they were waiting to tell her at the last minute.

'Is it going to be difficult for you?' Jake had picked up on her thoughts. Certainly, her father would be annoyed if she went there—he was already in a grumpy mood after she'd told him she was working with Nate, but she didn't see how she could get out of going to the event when she'd been roped in to open the proceedings on behalf of this year's charity—the Children's Unit.

'I think my biggest problem will be telling Dad,' she told him. 'He's already upset because Peninsula Holdings have sent out men to conduct land surveys on the estate—the tenancies could all be at risk—so any dealings I have with the Branscombes are likely to set him off.'

'Oh, dear.' Jake put an arm around her and gave her a hug. 'It's going to take a while for him to get over this latest blow, isn't it?'

'I think so, yes.' She nodded, comforted by the brief hug, until she looked up and saw with a faint shock that Nate had come into the room and was watching them, his green eyes assessing their clinch with obvious suspicion.

'Something wrong?' he asked.

Sophie eased herself away from Jake and braced her shoulders. 'Nothing I can't handle,' she said.

'That's always good to hear.' He studied Jake, his expression taut. 'Is there something we can do for you, Jake?'

Jake took a step backwards as if he was getting ready to move away. 'No, no…I'm looking for Tracey—I need her to road-test some equipment I've ordered from a new supplier. Trying to save money wherever, you know…'

'She's taken a child down to X-ray,' Nate said

curtly. 'I expect she'll be on her way back from there by now.'

'Oh, okay, thanks…I…I'll go and find her.' Jake raised a hand in a goodbye gesture to Sophie and headed for the exit doors.

'He's doing his best for this hospital, you know,' Sophie said, her blue eyes narrowing on Nate. He wasn't being uncivil towards Jake, but there was a definite friction in the atmosphere.

'Yeah, I know.' His green gaze lingered on her, dark and unfathomable.

She frowned. 'But you seem to have a problem with him…?'

'Mmm…you could be right…' His glance shimmered over her. 'It's what he's doing for you that bothers me.'

Her mouth made a faint wry quirk. Her relationship with Jake was none of Nate's business…but it kind of made her feel warm inside to know that he might be just a bit jealous. Perhaps he did actually care for her, deep down. Would there ever be a chance his feelings went further, and that she and Nate might get together? A strange tingling sensation started to run up and down her spine at the thought.

She gave herself a mental shake. She really couldn't afford to explore that notion, could she?

'Perhaps we'd do better to concentrate on the job in hand?' She gave Nate the file she'd been reading. He studied her, his eyes dark and brooding, but she ignored that and commented instead on the patient's folder. 'I'm concerned about Josh Edwards. I don't think the medication alone is going to be enough to resolve the situation,' she said. 'I think we should get him up to Theatre so he can be fitted with a drainage tube to relieve the pressure inside his head. The steroids and diuretics on their own aren't going to keep things under control.'

He glanced through the file and came to a swift decision. 'Okay. Notify the surgeon and ask Hannah to prep the boy.'

'Do you want me to talk to the parents?'

He shook his head. 'No, I'll do it. You might want to go and talk to the little girl with the belly piercing—she was asking for you.'

'Was she?' She smiled. 'From what she was saying yesterday, I expect she wants me to reassure her that there won't be a scar and that she can eventually go back to wearing crop tops. I looked in on her earlier this morning, but she was sleeping peacefully. The antibiotics seem to be dealing with the infection at last.'

'That's good. It's always nice to know when the treatment's working.'

'It is.' She glanced at him. 'Is there any news about your father? Is he making any progress?'

His mouth flattened. 'It's going to take time, I think. The heart attack caused damage to the heart muscle and he's finding rehab a strain. I'm booking him into a convalescent home so that he can rest and get the help he needs. We'll be transferring him there on Friday, so I should be able to check on him on Saturday morning and still do the honours at the fête in the afternoon. I've said I'll call out the winning raffle numbers.'

She nodded. 'I only heard about the change a little while ago. Jake was telling me that you're letting the organisers use the Manor. Aren't you worried about the damage that might be done to the grounds—your father's always been very particular about the way they look?'

'Not really. He's left everything up to me, and as far as I'm concerned, the old saying is true—what the eye doesn't see, the heart won't grieve over... Anyway, we have skilled groundsmen who know how to put things right afterwards. I'm more worried that villagers might boycott the event because of everything that's been in the newspapers about my father and the estate. There's been a lot of bad feeling, and word soon gets around. It would be a shame if that happened—it would be good to raise money for the Children's Unit. I certainly wouldn't want to jeopardise that in any way.'

'I don't think you need have any worries on that score. Everyone wants to contribute—I know a lot of people have been working very hard to try to make sure it's a success.'

'Well, let's hope it all turns out okay.' His gaze moved over her. 'I'll see you there, I hope?'

She hesitated, thinking about the implications of

that, and his gaze darkened. 'Yes,' she said. 'I'll be there to represent the Children's Unit.'

'I suppose Jake will be with you?'

She shook her head. 'He has to go to a meeting with some ex-colleagues in Cornwall, so he cancelled on me. But I'll have Charlie with me. I've entered him in the dog show, and I'm just hoping he'll walk properly on the lead and not show me up! He gets excitable if there's a lot going on. He might try to head for the flower borders if I don't keep a tight hold on him.'

He grinned. 'Oh, I can imagine… Charlie's quite a character, isn't he? I remember when he was a pup I was back home for a couple of weeks in the summer, and he dug up the lawn at the back of the Manor. My father was apoplectic when he saw a dozen or so holes appear in his pristine turf, but I couldn't help seeing the funny side. Your father was chasing Charlie, trying to stop his antics, but Charlie thought it was all a good game and kept stopping to dig a bit more. As soon as your father caught up with him, he ran off. The more he was chased, the more fun it was.'

Sophie rolled her eyes. 'He's always been a handful. But hopefully he'll behave himself on Saturday. At least he's grown out of digging holes.'

He smiled. 'I'm glad you're going to the fête.' A gleam of anticipation sparked in his eyes. 'I'll look forward to seeing you there.'

A quiver of nervousness started in the pit of her stomach. 'Yes, you too.' She set her mind on her work and went off to sort out the arrangements for Josh's operation.

To her relief, everything went smoothly. The neurosurgeon treated the request as an emergency and the little boy was whisked up to Theatre. Once there, the surgeon implanted a small silicone tube into the subdural space in Josh's head to draw off blood that was forming there, and the pressure on the little boy's brain was instantly lessened.

Sophie went home that day feeling much happier about his progress. Josh was still sedated for the moment, but she knew he stood a much better chance of recovery.

The day of the fête arrived—a gloriously sunny afternoon—and Sophie set off early with Charlie to walk to the Manor. Their route took them along the cliff top, with moorland stretching away into the distance. Soon, Branscombe Manor came into view, situated high up on a hill, looking out over the landscape, a beautiful yellow stone mansion formed in an elongated U-shape with two gable-ended wings making the U. Over the years there had been side extensions added towards the back of the house, again with magnificent gable ends.

The house was architecturally superb, with stone mullioned windows fitted with leaded panes. The glass sparkled in the sunlight and she paused to gaze at the house in wonder as she approached it from the long curving driveway. But then her attention was distracted by the arrival of a large white catering van turning in off the lane.

There would be burgers and hog roasts and all manner of refreshments laid on for the hungry visitors. Stalls had been set up on the sweeping lawn at the front of the building, with striped marquees to one side where people could sit at tables and enjoy a cup of tea or coffee. Further along she saw another marquee where alcoholic drinks were being served.

Sophie looked around. As a teenager, she'd come here often with her father, helping him as he carried out various tasks around the Manor. All those memories came flooding back now, as she gazed once more at the imposing house and well-tended gardens. At the side of the house there was a walkway through a stone arch that led to a rose garden and beyond that there was a land-scape of trees and shrubs.

'Hi, Sophie. Things are looking good, aren't they? We've a great crowd here already.' Tracey greeted her cheerfully, her fair hair tied up in a ponytail, her grey eyes lighting up as she saw Charlie. She bent down to stroke him. 'Shall I take him for you while you go and do the hon-ours?'

'Oh, bless you. Thanks, Tracey.' Sophie handed over the dog, who went willingly, pleased to be fussed and patted and generally crooned over. His tail wagged energetically.

Sophie stepped up on to the dais and set about formally opening the proceedings. 'We want you to have a great time here today,' she told everyone. 'We've all kinds of fun things for you to see and do this afternoon—there's face painting for the children, a karate demonstration taking place in the South arena at two o'clock, and music from our favourite band all afternoon. Don't forget to look in on the flower and plant marquees while you're here, and there are all sorts of cakes, jams, pickles and chutneys for sale in the home produce section. Above all, remember that any money you spend here will go towards buying much-needed equipment for the Children's Unit at the hospital. Please—enjoy yourselves.'

'Well said. That's the aim of the day.'

Sophie glanced around, her stomach tightening in recognition as she saw that Nate was waiting to take his turn on the stand. He looked good, wearing casual chinos and a crisp open-necked shirt that revealed a glimpse of his tanned throat.

Gesturing to him to come and take the microphone from her, she introduced him to the crowd and then stepped down. The atmosphere changed almost immediately as he took to the stage. People weren't sure how to react to him—it was clear in the silence that fell over them and in the way their expressions changed from smiling to sombre. His father's poor investments and lack of judgement had come down to haunt the son.

'Thank you, Sophie,' Nate said. He looked briefly at Charlie, who was busy trying to wind his lead around Tracey's legs in his efforts to get back to his mistress, and then he looked out at the sea of faces. 'Ah...I should mention there's a dog show too, for any of you who haven't yet had time to glance through your programme. It'll be held in the East Meadow at two-thirty.' He looked bemused as Tracey swiftly tried to untangle herself and Charlie began to pull her exuberantly towards Sophie and a child who was licking an ice cream.

'Among other things, there will be an obedience training exercise. I'm not sure if Charlie here will be a good candidate for that—he might be considered a bit of a disruptive element.' There was a ripple of laughter among the crowd as Charlie's ears pricked up at the mention of his name. The dog quickly turned tack, heading up on to the dais, pulling Tracey along with him. Worried, Sophie followed.

Nate grabbed hold of the leash from a relieved Tracey and then wound it firmly around his palm. 'Of course, he might do well in the sledge-pulling event.' Another murmur of amusement. He looked at the overexcited dog and said briskly, 'Charlie—sit!' To Sophie's amazement, Charlie sat, looking up at Nate with an expectant, adoring expression.

'Okay...' Nate turned his attention back to the audience. 'I'll call the raffle results at the end of the afternoon—we've a television as first prize, a hamper to be won, bottles of wine, and a whole array of wonderful things which you'll see on display when you buy your raffle tickets. Go and have a great time.'

Nate stepped down from the stage, bringing Charlie with him. 'Are you okay, Tracey?' he asked.

The nurse nodded. 'I just feel a little silly, that's all. I didn't expect him to go racing off like that.'

'I'm sorry,' Sophie said. 'Perhaps obedience classes would be a good idea, after all—except he's probably a little too old for them by now.'

'That's up for debate,' Nate said, laughing.

Tracey walked with them for a while as they wandered around the stalls and checked out the games on offer. Sophie tried spin-the-wheel and won a cuddly toy. 'That's one for the Children's Unit,' she said happily, holding on to the golden teddy bear. At the first opportunity she would pass it on to one of the organisers.

Nate had a go on the rifle range and hit the prime target, sending a spray of water to fall on Charlie's head. The dog promptly shook himself and showered everyone in the vicinity. 'Aargh, I'm sorry,' Sophie said, pulling the Labrador away.

'My fault,' Nate commented with a smile. 'I might have known he would try to get his own back.'

Tracey met up with a friend and went off with her to buy candy-floss, leaving Sophie and Nate to walk round the rest of the stalls together. They bought burgers from a van and walked along, eating them as they went. It was fun, until they began to be interrupted by villagers who stopped Nate and asked him about the tenancies on the estate and about the activities of Peninsula Holdings.

'What's going to happen to my home?' one man wanted to know. 'This company—Peninsula Holdings—has been sending men to measure up and ask a lot of questions. My tenancy's up for renewal in a few weeks. It always used to go through automatically, but what's going to happen now? Am I going to be put out of my home? Where am I going to go with my family?' He was understandably angry, disgruntled by the way things were going, not knowing how to plan for the future.

'Like I've told everyone else who's asked,' Nate said, 'nothing's been decided yet. Peninsula Holdings are looking into things to see if they want to do a deal. I may decide it isn't going to work. In any case, no one's going to be turned out at a moment's notice. It could be that you can go on renting, or any new buyer might want to offer the properties up for sale, but you would be given first option to buy. In any event, we'll make sure you're offered alternative accommodation.'

'And what if I don't want it? What if I don't want to move away? We've lived here in the village, in this house, all our lives.'

'I know…and I'm really sorry. I understand this is a difficult time for you.' Nate tried to soothe him, to calm all the people who came to complain or ask about what was going to happen, but nothing he said could appease them. Sophie could understand how they felt. It was all so unsatisfactory, with everything left up in the air, but she sympathised with Nate. She didn't see how he could tell them anything different if he was still awaiting the outcome of negotiations.

They headed over to the East Meadow for the dog show and watched the dog trials taking place. Sophie sighed. 'They're all so clever, aren't they, listening to what their owners say and going where they tell them to go?' She glanced at Charlie, who was panting, eager to get involved. 'Not so with this one, though,' she said with a smile.

Nate chuckled. 'He's one of a kind,' he said, tickling Charlie's silky ears. 'I think dogs need to listen if they're to learn, but he's never seemed to have that connection between ears and brain.'

She laughed. 'Oh, well, here goes… It's the competition for the best-looking dog—that's one thing he *is* good at. He's always been beautiful to look at.'

He watched her get ready to walk the dog over to the line-up. 'You make a perfect team,' he said. His glance shifted over her slender figure, neatly clad in blue jeans and a sleeveless top. She was wearing her hair loose, the curls tumbling down over her shoulders.

Unexpectedly, he took his phone from his pocket and swiftly took a photo. 'Two beautiful blondes.' He looked at the image on the screen and a glint of satisfaction came into his eyes. Sophie was oddly still for a moment, the breath catching in her throat at the casual compliment. Then she collected her thoughts and set off with Charlie, conscious all the time of a warm glow starting up inside her.

She came back to Nate a few minutes later, but there was no rosette to show for their efforts. 'I can't believe you were outshone by an Afghan hound,' she told Charlie. 'Don't let it bother you— you're way better-looking than any dog here.'

Nate smiled. 'Better luck next time, maybe.' He glanced at Sophie, his expression sobering. 'I'm still being pounced on from all sides. Shall we try and get away from here for a bit, before any-one else comes up and tries to waylay me? Have you seen everything you want to see for the time being?'

'Yes, okay. Where do you want to go?'

'I thought we might take Charlie for a walk by the river—that might wear him out for a bit.'

She smiled. 'Okay. I think he'll definitely be up for that.'

They left the meadow and walked along a foot-path until they came to the riverbank. The water was fairly deep at this point, flowing freely on its downward tilt towards the sea. It was fed by

the lake in the grounds of the Manor, a favourite
beauty spot when she had been a teenager. The
lake was on private land belonging to the Branscombes and was supposed to be out of bounds,
but she and her friends had often gone for walks
there on hot summer days. Further along, she recalled, there was a weir, where they'd stood and
watched the water tumble over stone and form
white froth.

'You must love this place,' she said now, watching the ducks glide on the water, dipping their
beaks every now and again among the reeds as
they searched for morsels of food. 'It's so peaceful and unspoilt.' They were following a well-
worn path by the river, where clumps of yellow
fleabane grew along the banks and here and there
were shiny deep pink blooms of musk mallow and
star-shaped ragged robin. Charlie was sniffing
among the blades of grass, seeking out the flower
petals and sneezing when they tickled his nose.

'I do.' He sent her a sideways glance. 'It's even
better having you here to share it with me.'

'Is it?' She was pleased but looked at him curiously. 'I wasn't expecting to see you at all outside of work, but I suppose when you opted to have the fête on the Manor grounds you felt you had to put in an appearance.'

'That's true...but I'd have turned up anyway, just so that I could spend some time with you.'

'Really?' Flattered though she was by his persistence, she wasn't about to fall for his charm the way countless other girls had in the past. 'That might have been awkward if Jake had been around.'

'Ah, but he isn't here, is he?' His eyes glittered. 'What was he thinking, choosing to go to a meeting and missing out on the chance of being with you?'

Impishly, she decided to play him along. She'd never said there was anything going on between her and Jake, but Nate seemed concerned about their relationship. 'He's very passionate about his work.'

'More than he is about you?' His dark brows rose in disbelief. 'Doesn't he know he's leaving you open to being chatted up by the likes of me?'

She smiled. 'We're just friends.' She sent him a fleeting blue glance. 'Besides, there's so much history between our families...'

'Yes, there is,' he said, trying to ignore the elephant between them. He checked his watch, a stylish gold timepiece that looked good on his strong tanned wrist. 'We've an hour or so left before I have to call the raffle results—we could go back to the house and get Charlie some water and I could show you round, if you like? You've never seen the inside of the Manor, have you?'

'Only the lodge, where my father had his office.' She smiled. 'I think I'd like that. I've always wondered what such a grand house was like inside.'

'Come on, then. We can take a shortcut from here across the field to the back of the house.'

He showed her the way along a narrow path that led to a hedgerow and a wooden stile. He held Charlie's lead while she swung her jeans-clad legs over the railing and stepped down into the field beyond. From here she caught a glimpse of the Manor House through the thicket of ancient trees that surrounded it.

'Are we going in through the servants' entrance?' she asked with a mischievous smile as they approached the back of the house. There were no stalls set up out here, and there was no sign of people coming away from the main event and wandering about. She guessed he'd had it temporarily fenced off.

'There's no servants' entrance nowadays,' he said, 'but it's not quite as grand as the archway at the front of the house.'

'Oh, I don't know about that…' She gazed at the covered portal. 'It's quite impressive.' The lawn and gardens here were beautiful, with wide flower borders and tall trees and a verdant shrubbery. Sophie went with Nate into the house through a pair of wide, solid oak doors and then stopped to look around in wonder.

She was standing in the kitchen, a huge room with gleaming pale oak floorboards and golden oak units all around. There was a large central island bar with a white marble top, and to one side there was a dining table with half a dozen chairs set around it. Above the range cooker there was

a deep, wide cooker hood with a tastefully de-
signed tiled splashback. All along one wall were
feature windows with square panes and two of
the windows were decoratively arched. The room
was light and inviting—it was the most wonderful kitchen she had ever seen.

'Oh, I'm almost speechless,' she said, gazing
around. 'I wasn't expecting anything like this. It's
so traditional, yet completely modern.'

Nate smiled. 'I persuaded my father a couple of
years back that it needed updating. I'm pleased
that for once he took note of what I said.' He
went to the sink and poured cold water into a
large stainless-steel bowl and set it down on the
floor for Charlie. The dog drank thirstily and
then flopped down on the tiles, watching them,
his head on his paws. 'What would you like to
drink?' Nate asked Sophie. 'Something cold, or
tea, coffee…? Something stronger, if you like?'

'A cold drink would be lovely, thanks. It's so
warm today—it's left me with a real thirst.'

'Watermelon?'

She nodded and he took two glass tumblers

from a display cabinet and filled them from a dispenser in the front of the tall double-door fridge. 'This is a mix of watermelon, a dash of lime and a hint of cucumber,' he said. 'I think you'll like it.'

She took the glass and swallowed deeply. 'Mmm...that's lovely. Thank you.'

'You're welcome.' He finished off his drink, tipping his head back. Sophie watched, fascinated as his throat moved, but she lowered her gaze as he put the glass down on the table. 'I'll show you the rest of the house,' he told her, 'the main part, at least. It would probably take too long to go through the East and West Wings.'

'Okay.'

There were several reception rooms, one used as a library and another as an office, all tastefully furnished with the same pale oak used in carved, decorative panelling on the walls and in the bookcases and desks. The drawing room, though, facing out on to a paved terrace, was very different.

'We went for a much lighter touch in here,' Nate

said. 'There's no panelling, as you can see, but we chose a very pale silk covering for the walls.'

'It's lovely,' she murmured. 'It's all so restful.' She looked around. 'You've kept the original inglenook fireplace, but everything blends in perfectly.' The fireplace was a pale stone arch with a wood-burning stove set into the recess. There were two cream sofas in here, with splashes of soft colour in the cushions and in the luxurious oriental design rug and floor-length curtains. Again, the windows were tall, with square panes, and there were glazed doors opening out on to the terrace.

'I'm glad you like it.' He smiled. 'Let me show you upstairs.' They went out into the large hall, almost a room in itself, and Sophie looked up to see gleaming pale oak rafters and a mezzanine floor set off by a beautifully carved oak balustrade. 'I have my own office up there,' Nate said, following the line of her gaze. 'I like to sit up there in the room and look out over the moors. You can see the lake from there, and a good deal of the estate. Come on, I'll show you.'

He reached for her hand and led her up the wide staircase to the open balcony that looked down on to the hall. His fingers engulfed hers and instantly she felt a thrill of heat pass through her at his firm touch.

The room opened out on to the internal balcony. There were a couple of easy chairs up here, with bookcases to hand along with a small glass coffee table. She imagined him sitting here, reading and being able to look down into the hall when anyone arrived downstairs.

Further back in the room, through a wide, square archway, there was a bespoke furnished study, with a built-in desk and units and glazed square-paned display cabinets above them. The main features, though, were the two wide arched windows that took up a good part of the back wall.

'Come and see.' Nate took her with him to stand by one of the windows. 'See what I mean?' He slipped his arm around her waist, holding her close. She knew she ought to move away but it felt good to have him hold her, to have him so close that she could feel his long body by her side, and she couldn't bring herself to break that contact. Instead, she wanted him to wrap his arms around her. His nearness was intoxicating.

'Oh...it's incredible!' She gasped softly in delight. 'You're so lucky to have such a wonderful view.' From here, with the house situated at the top of the hill, she could see all around for miles. She saw the lake and the copse, and beyond that she glimpsed some of the houses beyond, white-painted and nestled into the hillside. She looked at him, her lips softening with enchantment. 'It's all so lovely. I've never seen it set out like this before.'

'*You're* lovely,' he said huskily, his gaze lingering on the pink fullness of her mouth. 'It means so much to have you here with me like this. I've missed you, all those years we've been away from each other. I kept thinking about you all the time we've been apart.'

'Did you? Me too...' It was true. She'd never been able to stop thinking about him. And now she was lost in his spell, enticed by the compelling lure of his dark eyes and mesmerised by the gentle sweep of his hands as they moved over the curve of her hips, drawing her ever closer to him. He bent his head to her and gently claimed her lips, brushing her mouth softly with his kisses. Her whole body seemed to turn to flame and she melted into his embrace, loving the way his arms went around her. Her limbs were weak with longing. She wanted his kisses, yearned to know the feel of his hands moving over her.

'I've been desperate to kiss you ever since I saw you that day at the Seafarer,' he said, his voice roughened with desire. 'I wanted to hold you, to feel your body next to mine.'

She felt the same way about him, but his words made her stop and think about what she was doing. Her father had been upset when he'd heard about that meeting. He'd warned her about falling for Nate all over again. They'd never made any commitment to one another but, whenever he was around, she was drawn to him like a moth to a flame and, even though they'd argued, she'd been upset when he went to work in the States after her father's accident. How would she feel when his job here came to an end and there was the possibility of him leaving once more? It was better, surely, not to let things get out of hand?

'I wanted it too, Nate, but…I can't let this happen. I'm sorry if I led you on in any way. I'm very confused right now. I need time to think…'

'Why, Sophie? Tell me why.'

She looked up at him. 'I know you're not right for me,' she said quietly. 'It would be madness if I were to fall for you…again. We're worlds apart.'

'You don't know that.' His hands circled her waist. 'You seem absolutely perfect to me. I'd do everything I could to make you happy.'

She shook her head. 'But you can't. And what you're going to do will hurt my family and friends. Think about what you're doing—you're planning to sign away the homes of everyone who lives in property belonging to the Branscombe estate. It's no use saying you haven't made a decision yet. It's what you'll do to make sure that you can keep this house, isn't it? I understand that—the Manor has been in your family for generations; you said so. But do you really know the pain you will cause?'

He ran his hands lightly over her bare arms. 'If it came to that, if I have to sell the properties, I could negotiate a deal for you so that you could buy your house for a rock-bottom price.'

'And my father's home? What will happen to that? Can you tell me it won't be demolished to make way for a hotel or shopping mall? Isn't that what that company does? Will anything be left of our lovely tranquil village when they've finished?'

He winced. 'I'll make sure that your father gets a better place. He won't suffer.'

'He's already suffering. He's only just getting used to going around in a wheelchair and negotiating ramps. The last thing he needs is to be uprooted all over again.' She sighed heavily. 'It's as though you're moving chessmen on a board, deciding their fate.' She gazed searchingly at his face, studying the taut line of his jaw and the bleak sea green of his eyes. 'Nate, isn't there anything you can do to stop this?' She lifted her hand to his chest and ran her palm lightly over the warmth of his ribcage. 'Can't you find another way? Please?'

For a moment, his expression was agonised. 'I wish I could, Sophie, but a place like this, with all the land and outbuildings associated with it, costs a fortune in upkeep. I'll do what I can. You know I'd do anything not to hurt you.'

'I know you will. But things don't always work out the way we want them to, do they?' She eased herself away from him and took a couple of steps backwards. 'It's getting late. There's the raffle to draw and I should go and see what Charlie's getting up to. It's time we set off for home. He should be rested well enough by now. Thanks for showing me around.'

He walked with her to the kitchen. 'I could take you home in the Range Rover. Charlie could go in the back.'

'No, it's all right. We'll walk.' She needed to be alone right now, away from him, so that she could clear her head. With him around, it was impossible.

CHAPTER FOUR

'HI, JAKE. HOW did your weekend down in Cornwall go? Did things work out all right for you?'
Sophie walked into Jake's office at lunchtime on
Monday, greeting him with a bright smile. She
was glad to see him. He was a calming influence—everything Nate was not.

She should never have gone back to the Manor
House with Nate. That had been a big mistake,
and she might have known he wouldn't be one
to miss an opportunity. After all, he had nothing to lose.

Even now, she remembered how it had felt to be
in his arms, to know the touch of his lips on hers.
Her whole body tingled with nervous excitement
at the memory.

'Oh, hi, Sophie.' Jake looked up from the mound
of paperwork on his desk. 'Yeah, it went okay,

thanks. We managed to get quite a lot sorted.' He frowned. 'The hotel was a bit crowded, though. There was some sort of event going on in town— a music festival—so it was quite noisy.'

'But it must have been good to meet up with your friends?'

He nodded. 'Yes…yes, it was.'

She hesitated momentarily. He seemed harassed and out of sync with things, not at all his usual self. 'I came up here to see if we might have lunch together?' she suggested. 'Maybe you can tell me all about it over a plate of spaghetti?'

He frowned again, glancing at his watch, and then started shuffling through papers. 'I'm sorry, Sophie. I've a stack of work to wade through and I have to get a report ready for a meeting with my boss this afternoon. Do you mind if we give it a miss and meet up later?'

'No…no, of course not… That's all right.' She tried to hide her disappointment. 'It was just a spur-of-the-moment thing…I hadn't heard from you, so I thought I'd come and see you on the off chance. It doesn't matter.'

'Ah, yes… I should have phoned you. Every-thing's been a bit hectic.' He grimaced. 'How about I give you a call when I'm free?'

'Yes, okay. That's fine. No worries.'

She had plenty of other things to occupy her mind when she went back to the Children's Unit after grabbing a quick bite to eat in the hospital restaurant. She checked up on her patients, tak-ing time to look in on Josh, the five-year-old boy with the head injury, and she was thankful that his condition was at least stable now. He was still under sedation while they waited for the frac-tures to begin the healing process and while the swelling inside his head subsided. His parents were obviously worried about his prognosis and whether he would be brain damaged in any way, but Sophie reassured them as best she could be-fore going in search of her next patient.

As she was walking by a side ward, though, she heard a series of monitor alarms going off. Instantly concerned, she looked into the room to see what was happening.

Nate was in there looking after a young girl

who appeared to be around ten years old. When Sophie walked further into the room, she could see that the child was thrashing around on the bed, her limbs moving uncontrollably, her head tipped back and her body arching. She was having a full-blown seizure and Sophie hurried over to Nate and said quietly, 'Can I help?'

He nodded, giving her a quick smile. 'Thanks, I'd appreciate that. The nurses are all very busy just now... Would you try to hold her still while I give her a shot of anti-convulsion medication? She only just seemed to come out of one seizure and now this...'

'Of course.' Sophie gently restrained the child while Nate drew up a syringe and inserted it into the intravenous cannula that was taped to the girl's arm. 'Are her parents around?'

'Her father had to leave to go to work. I sent her mother to take a break and get some coffee. These last few weeks have been a worrying time for her and she's stressed out. Luckily, she missed seeing these latest seizures.'

'Do we know what's causing them?'

He nodded. 'I think so. Lucy has been suffering from really bad headaches, nosebleeds and vomiting for some time now. Her blood pressure's frighteningly high—it's been getting steadily worse over a couple of years despite treatment. It isn't responding very well to antihypertensive drugs.' He withdrew the syringe and put it aside. Glancing briefly at Sophie once more, he said, 'It might be a good idea if you were to stay with us while I explain things to her mother. She's quite upset by what's happening to her daughter, and it might help her to have another woman present. I'll need to get her consent for angiography.'

'All right, I can do that.'

Slowly, as the drug took effect and as Lucy recovered consciousness, Nate began to speak to the child in a low voice, soothing her and trying to keep her calm. Even Sophie began to feel more relaxed under the comforting influence of his gentle tones.

'How do you feel?' he asked the girl after a while. 'Is your headache still as bad as before?'

'No, it's a bit better.' Lucy was silent for a moment and then her face suddenly paled, small beads of perspiration breaking out on her brow, and she said urgently, 'But I'm going to be sick again.'

Sophie quickly found a kidney dish and held it for the little girl while she vomited, and then gave her a tissue so that she could wipe her mouth when she was finished. 'I'll just get rid of this,' Sophie said, removing the dish and replacing it with a clean one. 'I'll be back in a minute or two.'

When she came back into the room, Lucy was resting, leaning back against her pillows and looking completely washed out. Her dark hair was damp with perspiration. Her mother had come back from the cafeteria and Nate was sitting on the end of Lucy's bed, gently explaining the results of tests that had been carried out earlier. 'As you know, we've done lots of tests, along with ultrasound scans and a CT scan, and from those results we can be fairly certain about what's causing the high blood pressure.'

Lucy's mother frowned. 'You said it might be something to do with her kidneys.'

'Yes, that's right. From what we can see on the radiology films, the blood vessels to her kidneys are narrowed and that's what's causing the problems she's been having.'

'But you can fix it with tablets, can't you?'

Nate shook his head. 'I'm afraid not.'

The woman stiffened and Sophie pulled up a chair and went to sit with her at the side of the bed.

'There's some sort of blockage in the arteries,' Nate explained, 'and that is what's making her have high blood pressure and causing the severe headaches and so on. It also means that the blood flow to her kidneys is not what it should be. We have to do something that's more invasive, I'm afraid. If we don't do anything, things could get much worse and there might be damage to the kidneys.'

The woman's hands started to shake and Sophie covered them with her own, wanting to comfort her and at the same time not wanting Lucy to see her mother upset. 'We need to do a procedure called angiography,' she explained. 'This will clear the blockage and open up the arteries, but Lucy will be anaesthetised so she won't feel anything or need to worry about what's going on.' The little girl was watching and listening through all this, wide-eyed, and Sophie glanced at her. 'How do you feel about that, Lucy?'

Lucy paused briefly to think about it. 'Will it make me better?'

'It should do. That's what we're aiming for.'

Lucy was quiet for a moment or two, thinking about it. 'If it's going to help, I think it's okay.' Seemingly older than her years, she glanced at her mother and said, 'I'd like to stop feeling this way, being ill all the time.'

Slowly, her mother nodded. She exhaled heavily. 'All right. I'll phone your dad and explain things to him.' She looked up at Nate. 'When will you do it?'

'Tomorrow morning, most likely. I'll speak to the radiology consultant who'll be carrying out the procedure. He'll want to see Lucy, and he'll explain things to you…but basically he'll thread a catheter from the groin through the blood vessels to look at the kidneys. Then he'll place a small balloon inside the artery and inflate it to open up the blood vessel and restore the circulation. When that's been done satisfactorily, he'll withdraw the balloon and catheter. He'll need to do the process for both arteries.'

Lucy's eyes grew even wider. 'Are you sure I won't feel any of it?'

He nodded and smiled. 'I'm quite sure. You might feel a little bit sore at the injection site afterwards, but you'll be given painkillers, so it shouldn't be a problem.' He studied her expression. 'Are you still all right with it?'

She nodded.

'Good.' Nate stood up and smiled. 'We'll leave you to talk to your mum and dad about it, and I'll let the nurse know what's happening so she can answer any of your questions.'

'Thanks.' Lucy's mother smiled at both of them as they went to leave the room. 'I'm really grateful to you for the way you're looking after her.'

They went over to the computer room so that

Nate could type up his case notes and confirm things with the radiology consultant.

Sophie wrote up her own notes on Josh, and when they had both finished, Nate swivelled round in his chair to look at her. He said, 'I'm glad we've finally managed to catch up with one another. It's been so busy here we haven't had a chance to talk...but it was good being with you on Saturday. I wanted to tell you I enjoyed the whole afternoon, walking with you, spending time at the house...especially spending time at the house...' He smiled, but she couldn't be persuaded to do the same. She was still struggling with anxiety at her lack of self-control after the way she'd responded to him that day.

'It's certainly a beautiful house,' she said, dodging around the issue.

His mouth tilted at the corners. 'You won't admit you liked being with me, will you?'

'How can I?' She sighed. 'I feel I shouldn't have let things get that far.'

'I don't see why.' His shoulders moved in a nonchalant fashion. 'Anyway, it was just a kiss.'

She sucked in a silent breath at that. Just a kiss? Had it meant nothing to him? She was shocked.

'It was exquisite...sensational...wonderful...' he added. 'But it was just a kiss, after all. I don't see that you've any reason to regret it. It was instinctive. We didn't plan it. It just happened.' His glance flicked over her, moving from her burnished shoulder-length curls to glide down over the simple sheath dress she was wearing and trace the long line of her shapely legs. 'Though I wouldn't have been sorry if it had gone further.' His green eyes darkened. 'I always wanted you, Sophie...from back when we were teenagers. And I would definitely have staked a claim there and then if you hadn't decided to skip off to Medical School and disappear from my life for endless years.'

'Oh, really?' She pretended to be surprised. 'But you didn't try to find me, did you, and am I to believe you didn't go out and console yourself with any other girls in all those years?'

'If I didn't come after you it was because life got in the way. And as for any other women, trust me, no one could ever hold a candle to you.' All at once his expression was sincere, his gaze steady, and she almost faltered under the influence of that persuasive, utterly convincing guise until she managed to collect herself just in time. Was she a naive teenager?

'Well, that's good to hear.' She sent him a flashing blue glance. 'Although…you know I don't believe a word of it, don't you?' She frowned. 'There's no Irish in you, is there? I'm wondering because somewhere along the line you seem to have kissed the Blarney Stone.'

He tried to look offended but failed due to the faintly amused quirk of his mouth. His dark brows shot up. 'Not a drop. How could you say that to me? My ancestry is founded in the deepest combes—in the hills and valleys of ancient Devonshire—as you well know. I would never resort to such tactics.'

'Hmm. That's yet to be proved.' She pulled a wry face and might have said more but her phone rang and she unclipped it from the purpose-made jewelled clasp on the narrow belt around her waist. Then she glanced at the small screen and frowned. 'I'm sorry; I ought to take this,' she told him. 'It's my sister, Jessica. She almost never rings when I'm at work.'

'That's okay. Go ahead.' He was immediately serious but turned back to the computer while Sophie walked a short distance away to take the call.

'Oh, Sophie—' Her sister's voice came over the airwaves. 'I wasn't sure what to do—I didn't know whether to ring you or not. I don't know what to do.'

'It's all right—try to calm yourself.' Sophie used a soothing tone. 'I'm sure we can sort it out, whatever the problem is.' Intuitively, she asked, 'Is everything okay between you and Ryan?'

'Yes, except that he's had to go off to Canada on an engineering job—right now when my due date is so close.' Her sister pulled in a quick breath. 'I've been feeling so tired lately. I'm nearly full term, my back hurts, I'm getting these odd contractions—the midwife says they're Braxton Hicks—and he's away, working. It came up out of the blue and he said he had no choice but to go.'

Sophie tried to soothe her. 'I expect he's gone because he wants to boost your funds. Everything's been a struggle for you up to now, hasn't it, financially? He'd have known that Mum and Tom were close by if you needed them.' They hadn't counted on a baby coming along quite so soon.

'Yes, that's true. He's doing everything he can to make sure we're okay. It was all right till I had to stop working. I didn't realise how much we relied on my salary. We were doing all right, but then the boiler broke down and it's too old to be repaired, and now there's a problem with the plumbing that needs to be sorted but the plumber says he can't fix it for at least three weeks.' She sighed. 'I can't stay here but I don't know what to do. Can I come and stay with you for a while?'

'Oh, Jess…of course you can. Pack a case and catch the earliest train down here and I'll get the spare room ready for you. We'll book you in with a local midwife and arrange for you to have the baby in the local hospital. I'm sure everyone will be accommodating once we explain the situation.'

'Could I? Would you?' Jessica's words were

tumbling over themselves in her relief. 'Oh, thank you, Sophie. Thank you. Oh—' She broke off suddenly and Sophie could feel there was something more to come.

'What's wrong?'

'Well, it's nothing wrong, exactly, but I think Rob wants to come and stay with Dad for a while. You know what he's like once he makes up his mind about something. He's very impulsive. He keeps saying he wants to help look after him. Mum's okay with it, and I know Dad will be happy, but I don't know where he'll stay—Dad's spare room is being used for storage at the moment, isn't it?'

'I'm sure we'll sort something out.' Sophie tried to stay focused on the situation in hand. 'See if you can get the evening train over here. I think there's one that gets into town at about nine o'clock. I'll come and meet you at the station. We'll work out what we can do about Rob, but the priority is to get you settled first. You have to think about your health and about the baby.'

'Okay, I'll do that... Thanks, Sophie. You're

the best.' Jessica cut the call a minute or so later and Sophie frowned as she turned back to Nate, trying to work out what she needed to do. She would have to go home after her shift and make sure everything was ready for her sister.

'Trouble?' Nate was sympathetic, ready to listen.

'Not really. It's just that I need to get organised.' She explained what was happening with Jessica and how Rob wanted to come over.

'I don't see how she can stay on her own in those circumstances…but I'm sure she'll be glad to have her big sister's support.' He gave her a brief smile before asking seriously, 'Is there any way I can help out with Rob?'

It warmed her through and through to know that he would do what he could for her. 'I'm not sure, to be honest,' she said. 'But thanks for offering.' It was good of him—there had been no hesitation; he was ready to help in an instant.

She paused for a moment, thinking about what she was going to do. 'I won't be at all surprised if my mother turns up at my place some time soon.

This is just the kind of thing that would set her off. With all the changes going on, she'll probably forget to take her medication.'

He nodded. 'That could happen. She used to take off for days at a time, didn't she? I often wondered, back then, how you coped. You were only about sixteen when your parents' marriage broke up, as I recall, and your mother was in a bad way for a long time. I caught up with everything that was happening whenever I came home from Med School and Charlotte would phone me every week and let me know all the village news.' Nate's expression was pensive. 'Yet you seemed to take it all in your stride—you took on the role of mother to Rob and Jessica. They must have been...' he worked it out in his head '...seven and nine at the time?'

She nodded. 'That's right. They were very young, so I tried to be strong for them. It was hard because I was upset and hurting too. Dad was unhappy and not coping very well. It was still hard when Mum married Tom and we moved to

Somerset. It was a new life, a new place, but we felt as though our roots had been torn.'

'I can imagine.' His gaze narrowed thoughtfully. 'I don't suppose there's room for Jessica at your mother's place?'

She shook her head. 'When Jess married they turned her room into an office. Anyway, she craves peace and quiet—mentally, if not physically.' She shot him a quick, amused look. 'A bit like you, really. You'd never be able to put up with some of the organised chaos we live in.'

His mouth curved. 'Probably not. I'm used to things running smoothly, like a well-oiled machine. I suppose Charlotte had a lot to do with that.' He glanced briefly at his watch. 'Your shift's about due to finish—why don't you go home and make a start on getting things ready? It's going to be a bit of a squeeze for you in your small cottage, I imagine—and you'll need to make room for a cot in case the baby arrives in the next couple of weeks, won't you?'

'Oh, heavens! I hadn't thought of that! What am I going to do for a cot?'

He was thoughtful for a moment or two. 'There might be one stashed away in the attic back at the Manor. In fact, now I think about it, I'm sure there is. My father has things up there going back generations. He never throws stuff out.'

'Oh, bless you! That would be marvellous.' She studied him cautiously. 'Is there any news on your father?'

He pulled a face. 'There's been no change, really. He's being well looked after at the convalescent home, but his recovery's going to be a long haul, I think. He's very breathless and needs a lot of rest.'

'I'm sorry. It must be difficult for you.'

'Yes. Thanks for asking.' He sent her a quick glance. 'Is your father making any headway?'

She nodded, smiling. 'He managed to stand and bear his own weight for a short time. It's a start. He took a couple of steps with support. I'm keeping my fingers crossed that he'll keep on making progress.'

'I'm glad.'

She left the hospital a few minutes later, her

mind racing, full of things she had to do. It occurred to her that Jake had mentioned seeing her later, so she tried calling him. When he didn't answer, she sent him a text message telling him what was happening. He was probably in a meeting.

As soon as she arrived back at the village, she checked up on her father and heated up a beef casserole she'd made earlier.

'Rob told me he wants to come over,' he said as they ate together. 'I told him I'd love to have him stay with me but there's only the box room and that's filled with physio equipment and so on. It would take a bit of work to sort it out.'

'Don't worry about it, Dad,' she said. 'We can deal with that later.'

'And what about Jessica? Are you going to have room for her and perhaps for a baby as well at your place?'

'I'm sure we'll manage.' She looked at him thoughtfully. 'Anyway, how did you get on with the physio today—it was your day for the hospital workout, wasn't it?'

He grimaced. 'It was okay. I managed a couple of steps again, with a lot of help. Some days I don't seem to have the strength...'

'You're getting there—that's the main thing. A year ago we wouldn't have thought you'd come this far.' She clasped his hand warmly and smiled at him and he brightened, seeming to absorb some of her optimism. 'Now—I'll take Charlie for his walk and then I'll have to love you and leave you. I've a dozen things I need to do before Jessica gets here.'

Charlie's ears perked up at the mention of a walk and they set off along the moorland path, heading for the local village shop. Sophie stocked up on extra provisions and then dropped Charlie back home.

She went back to her own white-painted cottage and put away the groceries. With any luck, Jessica would be arriving in the next couple of hours and by then she would have everything more or less in order. She put fresh linen on the bed in the guest room and made sure there were plenty of clean towels in the bathroom. When she had finished it was still light, so she went out into the garden to breathe in the fresh air and gather some flowers from the border. She loved her garden with its curving lawn and pretty display of colourful blooms. There were trellis panels covered in sweet peas in warm pastel shades, with deeper lavender, mauve and blue colours interspersed.

The sun was setting on the horizon when she turned back towards the house, carrying a wicker trug filled with bright pompon dahlias and a posy of delicate sweet peas.

'I thought I might find you out here.' Nate's deep voice startled her. He walked around the side of the house and came across the small terrace towards her, smiling. 'I rang the doorbell and knocked, but I saw your car outside, so I guessed you were still at home. I brought the cot and came to see if you needed any help.'

'Oh...I didn't expect you to look for it right away.' She was a bit breathless all at once, seeing him standing there. He looked wonderful, dressed in casual chinos and an open-necked shirt with the sleeves rolled up. All the nervous excitement of the last few hours seemed to flow out of her as she looked at him, to be replaced by a warm feeling inside. It was so good to have him here.

'That's really thoughtful of you,' she said. 'It's good to see you, Nate.' She started towards the house once more, heading towards the open square-paned French windows. 'I was just going to put these flowers in water. Jessica likes sweet peas, so I thought I would put some in her room—and the dahlias will look good in the living room.' She was babbling, startled by his arrival, but thrilled to see him.

'Have you heard anything from your brother?' He followed her into the kitchen.

'No, nothing. I tried calling him but I couldn't get through. I expect his battery's low.' She set the trug down on the white table, then switched on the kettle and set out a couple of porcelain mugs for coffee. 'I'll just put these flowers in water. Sit down—I can get you some scones to eat if you're hungry.'

'No, thanks, I'm fine. Besides, you have enough to do without bothering about me.' He watched her as she arranged the sweet peas in a glass vase.

'Look—why don't I go and meet Jessica at the station? She'll remember me from before your family left the village—and we met up briefly in the village last time I was home.'

'Are you sure you don't mind doing that?'

'Of course not. I told you, I want to help.'

'Thanks. That would be such a relief. I'm really grateful.' She made the coffee and slid a mug towards him. 'I've been thinking about her, wondering if it will all go smoothly.'

He looked at her curiously. 'You don't show your feelings to the world, do you? You look very calm and composed on the outside, but I know you're a little anxious inside. That's probably what makes you such a good doctor. You get on with the job in hand—no panic, no fuss, just sheer concentration and doing the best you can.'

She gave a small broken laugh. 'You make me sound like a robot!'

'No! Never.' He stood up and laid his arm around her shoulders. 'It's all right to admit that you worry sometimes. I'm here for you, Sophie. I need you to know that.'

She reached up and touched his hand, and his fingers closed around hers. The warmth and gentle strength of that grasp encouraged her and somehow gave her a renewed burst of energy. With him around she could cope with anything. 'Thanks. I'm glad you're here.'

'Me too.' He released her and seemed to brace himself as though he was cautious about holding her for too long. Reading her thoughts, he said, 'Just being near you drives me wild. You can't imagine how difficult it is for me.'

'It isn't easy for me either...but, no matter what you say, I can't help feeling I need to keep my guard up. I don't want to fall for you, Nate. It's way too risky for my peace of mind.'

He looked at her, his dark eyes brooding. 'We need to work on that.' He started to walk away. 'I'd better go and get the cot—it's in the back of the Range Rover. There's a nursing chair as well—it rocks gently, so Jessica will be comfy when she feeds the baby.'

She went with him, following him out along the path to where he was parked at the front of the cottage. She didn't know quite what she was expecting—perhaps a very old, serviceable child's cot—but what she saw made her gasp with delight.

'Oh, it's lovely! I didn't realise it would be a crib that swings from side to side.' The white cradle had beautifully carved spindle sides and was supported on a sturdy white wooden frame. The rocking chair was a perfect match, white-painted with spindle legs.

Nate carried them into the house and put them down in the guest room she had prepared. 'There, the cot looks good next to the bed, doesn't it?' He studied it, looking pleased.

'Oh, it's just perfect. I never imagined you'd bring anything as lovely as this.'

'It was mine, apparently. I remember my mother talking about rocking me in a cradle at the side of the bed. She said it sent me off to sleep every time.'

'Thank you. I'm so grateful to you.' Forgetting everything, without thinking, she turned towards him and hugged him tightly. He was there for her when she needed him without her even having to ask. That meant a lot to her.

His arms closed around her, folding her to him in a warm embrace. 'You're very welcome. Any time.'

She looked up at him, his handsome face just inches away from her own. She felt safe in his arms. He only had to bend his head a fraction more towards her and their lips would be touching. A surge of longing swept over her, filling her body with aching desire.

His green eyes shimmered with answering passion and he slowly lowered his head. He breathed in raggedly. 'Sophie,' he said softly, 'you need to think about what you're doing, about what you want...because I'm just a man and I'm finding it really hard to resist you. I don't want you to blame me afterwards for anything that might happen between us.'

His gentle words brought her back swiftly to reality. What was she doing? She pulled in a shaky breath. 'Ah...I wasn't thinking. You're right. I'm sorry.' Her hands were trembling as she dragged herself away from him. 'I don't know what's wrong with me. I haven't been able to think straight ever since you came back. It's like I'm eighteen again, as though the intervening years count for nothing.'

His hand lifted, his fingers tangling in the soft mass of her silky curls. 'I wish we could go back too...I want to turn the clock back and start again, and this time no bad things would happen to tear us apart. If I could write my own story, I'd make it one where you and I could be together and nothing would come between us.'

She gave him a tremulous smile. 'That would be good, wouldn't it? But this is real life, Nate. It never seems to go smoothly for either of us, does it?'

He shook his head and slowly took a step back from her. 'No, it doesn't.' He straightened and said quietly, 'I should go and pick up your sister.'

'Yes...thanks.' She nodded, taking a moment to get herself together. 'I'll send her a message to let her know you'll meet her instead of me.'

After he'd gone, Sophie looked once more at the

room she'd prepared for her sister and the baby. She would have to buy bedding for the cradle, and maybe a mobile to hang above it, and she would find some soft cushions for the chair. They could be her gift for the baby.

It grew darker outside but there was no sign of Rob turning up and she busied herself with a few chores. At last the doorbell sounded and she opened the door to Jessica and Nate.

She greeted them with relief. 'Jessica, I'm so glad you're here.' She reached for her sister and put her arm around her. 'Come and sit down in the living room and put your feet up for a bit. You look exhausted.' Jessica's complexion was pale against the soft gold of her fair hair. Sophie glanced at Nate, who was following them along the hallway, and mouthed silently, 'Thank you.'

He smiled. 'I'll put the kettle on, shall I? I expect Jessica could do with a cup of tea…and maybe one of those scones you mentioned. From what she tells me, she hasn't been eating too well—too much heartburn lately.'

'Oh, it happens, doesn't it, when the baby gets

bigger and presses on everything? It must be horrible.' Sophie helped her sister into a cosy armchair and pulled up a footstool for her. 'Perhaps you need to snack little and often. I have some of your favourite strawberry jam to go with those scones.'

Jessica smiled, her pretty face lighting up. 'Oh, it's good to be here with you, Sophie. I'm feeling better already.'

'I'm glad to hear it. We'll get you sorted out with a midwife and so on tomorrow. For now, you just need to rest.'

Nate pulled up a small side table and set down a cup of tea beside her chair. 'Why don't you girls try to relax for a bit and enjoy being with one another? I'll leave you to it. I'm sure you have a lot of catching up to do.'

Sophie followed him along the hallway to the front door. 'Thank you for everything.'

'You're welcome.' He leaned forward and dropped a light kiss on her forehead before opening the door and walking swiftly down the path to his car. She watched him go, hoping that nothing would cause their new closeness to fall apart. It meant a lot to her that he was around.

But how was she going to square that with her father's feelings towards the Branscombes? He, of all people, had reason to be hostile towards them and he would worry in case she was hurt again.

CHAPTER FIVE

A SHARP RAPPING sound startled Sophie just a few minutes later. She finished stacking plates in the dishwasher and went to see who was knocking at the door.

She hurried along the hallway. Jessica had gone to her room, exhausted, and she didn't want her to be disturbed by the noise. She opened the front door.

'Hey, Sophie.' Seventeen-year-old Rob stood on the doorstep looking tired, sheepish and dishevelled, his fair hair spiky. 'Can I stay with you for a bit—just till I clear out the box room at Dad's house? I didn't want to tell him I was coming over. I wanted to surprise him.'

'Of course you can. Oh, come here—let me hug you.' She wrapped her arms around him and held him close for a minute or two. 'How did you get here?'

'I thumbed a lift with a couple of lorry drivers. But the last one dropped me off a few miles from here and I had to walk the rest of the way. Then Nate Branscombe saw me and offered me a lift.'

'Nate saw you?' she echoed. 'But he— Where is he?' He wasn't here with Rob and she couldn't see beyond the tall hedge that obscured the road.

Rob carefully extricated himself from her arms and tilted his head towards the front gate. 'He's cleaning the headlamps on the car—we went through a bit of muddy water.'

'Oh, I see.' Gathering her thoughts, she ushered her brother into the house. 'Go and make yourself a hot drink, Rob. There's food in the kitchen. I'll just go out and talk to Nate for a minute.' She frowned, a sudden thought occurring to her. 'Did you and he get on all right?'

'Yeah, I guess. I wasn't sure how to react to him but he told me you knew I wanted to be with Dad.' He winced. 'I know Mum doesn't want us to have anything to do with him—she still cares about Dad even though they're not together any more. She's always saying how Nate's father caused Dad to break his back, but I don't think Nate had anything to do with that. He always seemed okay to me—a bit of an 'us and them' divide, sort of, but okay. But I suppose you never know. He comes from a different world to us and things are passed down in families, aren't they? It's all in the genes—character traits, some kinds of illnesses and so on?'

'Sometimes. Go in and get warm. I'll be back in a minute.' She suspected Nate was cleaning the headlamps to give her and Rob some time to themselves but she wanted to thank him for finding her brother.

She went out to greet him. 'Hi there.'

'Hi.' Nate smiled in the darkness. A streetlamp lit up his features and she had to resist the impulse to put her arms around him and hold him close. She was so glad to see him, and so grateful that he'd taken the trouble to bring Rob home.

'Thanks for bringing my brother back to me,' she said. 'I'm overwhelmed, the way things are turning out. You must be tired by now. It's very late and we had a busy day at the hospital.'

'Yes, it is, but I'm okay.' He studied her, seeing that she was still dressed in jeans and a sweater. 'You're still up.'

'Yes, I wanted to make sure that Jess was comfortable. Do you want to come in for a coffee or tea or something?'

'Hmm...' He seemed to be thinking about that and his mouth curved. 'The "or something" sounds very tempting.'

Her cheeks flushed with warm colour. 'You know what I mean.'

'Yes...' He gave a soft, amused sigh. 'Unfortunately, I do.' He studied her, his eyes glinting, his gaze running over the tousled mass of her honey-blonde hair and the hot flare of her cheeks. 'I think, in order to avoid temptation, I'd better pass on the offer of a drink tonight. And, as you say, it's late.' He braced himself and came back to the matter in hand. 'Are you going to find space for Rob to bed down here?'

'He'll have to use the sofa.'

'I thought so. I offered to find him a room at the Manor House but he very politely refused. He said he didn't think it would be a good idea, given the way your parents feel about the Branscombes.'

'I'm sorry about that.' She pulled a face. 'He's probably right, though. If my dad found out, he would be very annoyed. I'd sooner not upset him right now or it could set his progress right back.'

He nodded. 'It's okay. I see your point. Actually, I think Rob will do better staying with you—he seems a bit down at the moment and I get the feeling he needs family around him. Too much going on in his life, perhaps…worries about college.'

She frowned. 'I know he wasn't enjoying the course he was on. I think he feels he chose the wrong subject. Or it may be something else altogether.'

'I'm sure you and Jessica will manage to help him get through it.' Nate smiled. 'I'll say goodnight, then, and leave you to go and look after your brother. I take it Jessica's okay? I told Rob she was here with you.'

'She's fine, thank you…and she absolutely loves

the cot and the chair. She was amazed when she walked into the guest room and saw them there. She wants to thank you personally for giving them to her but she asked me to tell you if I saw you in the meantime. I think she's probably fast asleep right now.'

'I'm glad she's all right.' He slid behind the wheel of the Range Rover and started the engine. 'Shall I see you back at the hospital in the morning?'

'Yes, I'll be there. See you.'

She watched him drive away and turned to go back into the house. She was pleased Rob was home, and even more glad to know that Nate had been the one to find him.

What she had to do now was send her parents messages to say that Rob and Jessica were both safe and sound with her. With any luck, they would read them first thing in the morning so she wouldn't have woken them.

She went back into the house and found pillows and a duvet for Rob. Like Sophie, he was exhausted, and after he'd had a meal of a hot Cornish pasty and soup, along with a hot drink, she helped him to settle in the living room.

'You can bed down on the sofa for now,' she said. 'It's quite comfortable, so all being well, you should be able to get some rest. We'll talk in the morning before I leave for work, and then maybe we'll be able to have a proper chat later on. Nate said you were feeling a bit low.'

Rob sat down on the sofa and pulled a face. 'I'm always up and down lately. Sometimes life seems black and empty and yet other times I'm on top of the world. I don't understand it.' He sent her an anxious look. 'Sometimes I worry that I might be bipolar, like Mum.'

She knelt down beside him. 'I don't think you need worry about that, Rob. We would have noticed signs before this if you suffered from the illness she has. I think what you're feeling is just part and parcel of being a teenager. Maybe we need to find a better way of supporting you.'

He nodded absently, absorbing that. 'I hope that's all it is.'

'Well, Jessica's here, so you'll be company

for each other—and it will make me feel better knowing you're here to keep an eye on her. You can let me know if she shows any sign of going into labour.'

His brows shot up and he said in a faintly alarmed tone, 'Is that likely to happen? She's not due yet, is she?'

'No...she still has a few days, possibly, but the baby seems quite big and there's not a lot of room for him in the womb, according to her last session with the midwife. Things could start happening any time.'

Rob looked worried and she laughed. 'It'll be fine, Rob. A first baby always takes a few hours, so there'll be no need to panic. Just ring me if anything seems to be starting.'

He nodded vigorously. 'I will—definitely.'

'Okay.' She smiled. 'Try to get some sleep.'

Despite having a disturbed night, Sophie was up early in the morning, preparing breakfast and getting ready for work. Rob appeared in the kitchen, bleary-eyed, as she was scrambling eggs at the hob, and he pulled out a chair by the table and sat down. 'Dad rang, didn't he?' He yawned and stretched his limbs. 'I heard him on the phone to you. You seemed to be trying to calm him down.'

'He wasn't happy because it was Nate who found you and brought Jessica here—he thinks I shouldn't have anything to do with him outside of work. I tried to explain but he wasn't really listening to anything I had to say.' She made a wry face. 'I suppose I'll still be in his bad books when I go round there to help out with Charlie. It'll give him another chance to have a go… But there was one good thing—he's really pleased that you're safe and sound.'

Rob gave a quick smile at that. Sophie guessed he missed living with his father. He went to see him as often as possible but that wasn't the same. 'I can give Dad a hand this morning if you want,' he offered. 'I know you normally have breakfast with him. It'll give me a chance to talk to him and I can take Charlie out for a walk, if you like.'

'Oh, that would be great, thanks. It will give me time to phone the midwife and sort things out before work. I'll let him know you're coming.' She was pleased he wanted to do that. It would do him good to talk to his father.

'Did I hear you say you were going to take Charlie for a walk? How about I come with you?' Jessica came into the kitchen, blonde hair gleaming, her expression showing her delight at being with her family.

'Yeah, why not?' Rob smiled a greeting and they all sat round the table, tucking into toast and perfectly cooked eggs. They talked about things that had been going on in their lives, but most of all it seemed that Rob and Jessica were relieved to be back home in the village where they were born.

'I've set up an appointment for you with the local midwife for tomorrow morning,' Sophie told her sister as she was getting ready to leave for work a short time later. 'She lives in the village, so she knows our family well. She's going to arrange things with the maternity unit at the hospital.'

'Thanks, Sophie.' Jessica patted her abdomen.

'I wish baby would hurry up—it can't be much longer, surely?'

Rob's eyes widened in momentary panic. 'Just don't have him yet, okay? Just leave it till the weekend when Sophie's around...yeah?'

'Of course, bro—whatever you say!' Jessica laughed and ruffled his hair. Smiling, Sophie said goodbye and left for the hospital.

She did the rounds of the Neonatal Unit and then went on to see patients who'd been admitted to the Children's Unit. Josh's condition was less critical now as his head injury healed, and Sophie and Nate had decided it was time to gradually reduce his level of sedation. They had to wait and see what the outcome might be as he slowly recovered consciousness, but Nate had said he wanted to check on him later today when they brought the boy fully out of his induced coma.

She and Nate had both been busy all day and hadn't had time to stop and talk, but she met up with him by the nurses' station late in the afternoon. He was holding out a newspaper.

'Have you seen this in the daily paper?' He

looked harassed and on edge, not at all his usual calm self.

'What is it?' She took the paper from him and scanned the article he'd been reading.

Villagers Protest about Homes up for Sale!

Peninsula Holdings are ready to make an offer for the Branscombe estate. Lord Branscombe, once involved in piloting a plane that crashed causing devastating injuries to his former Estate Manager, lost several millions of pounds in an ill-fated business venture overseas and now hopes to recoup his losses.

It's thought that he borrowed money to finance the investment. He suffered a heart attack recently and is now recovering in a convalescent home.

The villagers are seeking urgent talks with his son and heir, Nate Branscombe. Nate was unavailable for comment last night.

She sent him an anxious look. 'Is it true? Are the houses up for sale? Have you made a deal with Peninsula?'

'That's just it…I haven't spoken to the company yet. They finished their surveys last week and prepared a report for their head office. They're supposed to be getting in touch with me some time this week with a preliminary offer, but I've no idea what it will be.' His jaw tightened. 'They'd no right to leak this to the press and stir up trouble all over again.'

'What will you do?'

He pulled a face. 'The parish council has asked me to address an emergency meeting in the village hall later today. They've obviously been spooked by this article. I said I would do it providing there was no press intrusion, but I would have preferred to wait until I'd sorted things out. It all takes time—I have to meet with the accountants, try to set things up. They don't seem to realise that.'

She swallowed hard. 'I think people do understand…but everyone's nervous about the future. My own family's worried. I've just told Rob he can stay with me until we sort out better arrangements for him—he puts on an outward show of being okay but he needs stability. My dad said he can go and live with him once we clear out the spare room—but, even if he goes there, we don't know how long that set-up will be safe. They could both be uprooted before he has a chance to settle.'

'I told you, you don't have any reason to be concerned.' His mouth made a firm line and his green eyes were fiercely determined. 'I'll make sure the changes don't make things bad for you.'

She shook her head. 'I know you mean well, Nate, but once you sell out to Peninsula things could change. I'm sure their lawyers are clever enough to find ways to tear up any agreement. According to one of the men from the company, my dad's house will most likely be scheduled for demolition so they can build on the land. He's been worried about it ever since. Everyone's upset. No one knows how long they will be able to stay in their homes. Some people have lived in their houses since they were children. It's more than bricks and mortar that are at stake—it's the foundation of their lives.'

Nate cupped her shoulders with his hands. 'I do understand that, Sophie, and I'm doing my best to work things out…but there's a lot involved and it's not something I can do overnight.'

'I know.' She frowned. 'Perhaps it will help if you keep people updated with what you're trying to do. As things are, everyone's in the dark and coming up with worst-case scenarios.'

'I suppose you're right. I'll talk to them at this meeting.' His thumbs made soothing warm circles on her shoulders. It felt good and she wanted him to go on holding her, but he let his hands drop to his sides as Tracey appeared at the far end of the room.

She came over to the workstation and handed him a lab report. 'I thought you'd want to see this as soon as it came in,' the nurse said. 'It's the report on Lucy's angiography.'

'Ah, thanks, Tracey. That was quick.' Tracey smiled and walked away, leaving Nate to quickly read the lab's analysis. 'Apparently the treatment went well this morning,' he told Sophie. 'The blood flow to her kidneys has improved dramatically. There was a fibrous thickening causing an obstruction in both arteries, but that's been resolved now.'

Her mouth curved. 'It's all good, isn't it? When I looked in on her a little while ago, her blood pressure readings were getting back to normal. Do we know what caused the thickening in the first place?'

He shook his head. 'These cases are always difficult—there might be a genetic cause, but we can't know for certain. All we can do at the moment is try to put things right.' He glanced at his watch. 'It's getting late—there was an emergency with one of the patients and I missed out on lunch. Do you want to go and grab a coffee with me and maybe a snack?'

Her mouth turned down at the corners. 'I can't, I'm afraid. I said I would go and see Jake for a few minutes in my afternoon break. He's been so busy we haven't had time to get together for a while, but he sent me a text message this afternoon to see how things were going with Rob and Jessica. I think I need to let him know what's happening.'

A muscle flicked in his jaw and she guessed he wasn't happy about her seeing Jake.

She said cautiously, 'He and I are just friends, you know.'

'Hmm. Maybe.' Nate straightened. 'I'll see you later, then. Is there any chance you might come to the meeting at the village hall this evening? I'd like to have you there with me.'

She nodded. 'Yes, of course I'll go with you.'

She turned away to go and meet up with Jake, conscious all the time of Nate's narrowed gaze on her. Then Tracey came back and she heard her telling him about a problem that had cropped up with one of his patients, and he went off to deal with the situation. She guessed he wouldn't be getting the break he wanted.

Sophie took the lift up to the next floor. Jake would still be in his office. He'd told her earlier that he'd been busy all day, talking to suppliers and arranging new contracts.

'Sophie, it's good to see you.' His smile widened as she entered the room and he moved some of his paperwork to one side.

She gave him an answering smile. 'How are things going?'

'Oh, I've been deluged with work. The bosses want a lot of changes from the old system—more ways to save money and so on.'

'I suppose that's always going to be how things are. They're always trying to get a quart out of a pint pot. I don't envy you trying to make things work. You've put in a lot of overtime on this latest project, haven't you?'

'Yes, I have—it's taken a good deal of effort to put all this together.' He waved a hand over the files that were stacked up on his desk.

'Have you had time to eat? I could go to the cafeteria and bring you back some lunch if you can't get away?'

'Oh, that's okay—I went out to lunch with a couple of colleagues. We tried out the new restaurant by the river.' He glanced at her and said quietly, 'I'm sorry I haven't been there for you these last few days. You've a lot going on just now.'

'It's okay. You have, too.' She gave him a thoughtful look. 'You've been very busy.'

He frowned. 'Yes…yes…I was over in Cornwall again yesterday, talking to Cheryl and Matt about their systems and practices, or I'd have been in touch sooner.'

'Ah, yes, Cheryl…' Her brow creased as she tried to remember. 'I think I met her at one of the hospital's social functions. Nice girl. I seem to remember you liked her quite a lot.'

He looked at her oddly, seemingly nonplussed. Perhaps he'd thought she hadn't noticed. 'I… Well, she…'

She smiled. 'You'll have to let me know how things go with her.'

He shook his head. 'It's a non-starter. She only has eyes for someone else—a bit like you with Nate, I think…I can tell you both care for one another, but you must see that Nate never shows any sign of wanting to settle down. He's a heartbreaker, Sophie, and if he had his mind set on it, I dare say he would make a determined play for you. I suppose he's too involved with this estate business right now, though, and with his father being ill he's preoccupied.'

'That's probably true.' She started to walk towards the door. She didn't know what she thought about Nate, so she didn't want to talk to Jake about it just yet. 'I'll see you later, Jake.'

'I don't want to see you fall any further under his spell, Sophie. He already has you confused—I can tell. We should talk some more.'

'Yes, okay, we can do that. But I have to go now. I need to get back to work.'

'Shall I see you after work?'

'No, not today—I can't manage it. I have to go to a meeting at the village hall—about the estate being taken over. Tomorrow, perhaps.'

'Okay.'

She stopped to pick up a couple of coffees in disposable cups from the cafeteria, along with a pack of sandwiches for Nate. He'd said he hadn't eaten and he might appreciate some food.

Nate's expression was taut when she went back to the Children's Unit, and she wondered if he was still annoyed about the article in the paper and on edge about the meeting that was to take place later today. She approached him cautiously, not wanting to break into his introspection, but he acknowledged her with a brief nod.

'You weren't with Jake for very long,' he said, glancing up from the computer monitor where he was studying a series of CT images.

'No. We're both busy people,' she said. 'He just took a five-minute break.'

Nate seemed relieved. She pushed a coffee cup towards him and handed him the carton of sandwiches. 'I thought you might be hungry as you said you missed lunch.'

His eyes widened and he gave her a beaming smile. 'Bless you, Sophie. You're an angel.' He broke open the flip pack and bit into a chicken-and-mayo sandwich like a starving man. 'Mmm… this is great. Thank you—it was really thoughtful of you to do this.'

'You're welcome.' She turned the conversation back to work. 'You told me earlier that you wanted to look in on Josh before we finish here. Do you want to do that as soon as you've finished eating?'

He nodded. 'It's always a bit fraught, taking children off sedation after a head injury. I remember how it felt for me when I was a child, coming round a few days after my accident. I was intensely irritable and I didn't really understand anything that was going on. The nurses were great, though, incredibly patient.' He swallowed his coffee. 'My mother calmed me just by being there, talking to me and holding my hand. I don't remember what she said but it made me feel a lot better.' His features darkened momentarily as he recalled that time and for an instant his expression was bleak.

She wanted to reach out and hold him, to try to soothe his troubles away and make up for all the bad things that had happened in his life, but the fact that they were in a public place stopped her. 'It must bring back painful memories for you,' she said. He'd loved his mother and she'd been torn from him not too long after that.

'Yes, it does, even now.' He finished off his coffee and shrugged off his pensive manner. 'Let's go and see how Josh is getting along, shall we?'

'Okay.' She went with him to the side ward where they found Josh being looked after by Hannah. The five-year-old was agitated and restless, pulling at tubes and monitor cables, while his parents were looking on anxiously.

'What's happening to him?' his father asked, looking at Nate. 'Is this a sign that something's wrong?'

'Not at all.' Nate shook his head and drew up a chair so that he could sit down beside the parents. 'It's quite normal for a child to be agitated when he's coming off sedation. Hannah will make sure that he's comfortable and that he can't harm himself in any way. You don't need to worry—it looks alarming but, believe me, it's quite normal.'

He went on gently trying to reassure them. 'We need to check that he's not in any pain or suffering discomfort of any kind. Hannah will stay with him to see to that. We find it's best to keep everything reasonably quiet and dim the lights…but if you talk to Josh and try to encourage him, that might help to calm him down. He'll take a while to process information as his brain recovers, so don't expect a clear response from him just yet. You need to take things slowly.'

The man nodded. 'We will.' He reached out to hold his son's hand and spoke to him softly, and the little boy seemed to quieten at the sound of his father's voice. The child was very pale, his fair hair damp against his forehead.

After checking him over and conferring with Sophie as to his medication, Nate took his leave of the parents and thanked Hannah for doing a good job of looking after the child.

They started to walk back towards the desk but Nate's phone rang before they reached it. He listened carefully to the person at the other end of the line and then said curtly, 'Okay, I'll come over. Give me half an hour.'

He was silent and a bit grim-faced as he cut the call and Sophie said cautiously, 'Are you all right? Is something bothering you?'

He gave an awkward shrug. 'I just heard from the convalescent home that my father has taken a turn for the worse. He has a chest infection, so they have him on oxygen and high-strength antibiotics. I need to go and see him before I go to the meeting—it'll be a bit of a rush but I'll pick you up from your house at around a quarter to seven, if that's all right with you?'

'Yes, that's fine.' She laid a comforting hand on his arm. 'I'm sorry he's not doing so well.'

'Thanks.' He smiled at her and squeezed her hand in response. For a second or two he moved closer and bent his head towards her as though he might drop a kiss on her forehead, but at the last moment he straightened and gently disengaged his arm.

Sophie had to suppress an odd sensation of regret for what might have been. More and more lately, she found herself wanting closer contact with him. Instinct told her she could end up hurt and ultimately abandoned if she let herself get involved with him—his track record with women wasn't good but she couldn't help the way she felt.

She walked with him back to the computer station and prepared to go home. 'I'll see you later,' she said. 'I hope there's some good news about your father.'

'You too,' he answered. 'Good luck with Rob and Jessica. I imagine they're settling in all right?'

'I'm sure they'll be fine.'

She went home and phoned her father to make sure he was all right before hurrying to get changed for the meeting.

'Do you think Dad's still annoyed with you? How did he sound on the phone?' Rob asked. 'He's been on edge all day. Even Jessica had to try to calm him down. She took him a shepherd's pie a little while ago—it used to be his favourite.'

'It still is.' Sophie nodded. 'He told me to tell her how much he enjoyed it. Yes, he's still disappointed in me. I think he's also a bit apprehensive about this meeting tonight. He said he's going along to have his say. A friend's taking him.' She sighed. 'I wish the press hadn't stirred everything up. Nate says he's working on sorting things out but he needs time and no one's giving him that.'

'Well, good luck, anyway,' Jessica said. 'I'm glad I'm not going to be there to see sparks fly.' She had made dinner for the three of them and they sat round the table and talked for a while, enjoying being together.

Nate called for Sophie as he had promised. Jessica thanked him profusely for the cot and the chair, and Rob thanked him for giving him a lift to Sophie's house.

'I'm glad I was some help.' Nate gave them both a quick smile and then flicked a glance over Sophie, who was wearing a navy pencil-line dress teamed with navy stiletto heeled shoes. His dark brows shot up and he gave a silent whistle. 'Wow!' he said under his breath as they went out to his car. 'You look stunning.'

'Thank you.' She'd aimed to dress simply but stylishly for the occasion and she hadn't expected such a reaction from him. It felt good, though, to know that he thought she looked good. 'How is your father?' she asked.

He grimaced. 'He seems to be comfortable at the moment.'

They drove to the village green, where he parked his car near to the hall where the meeting was due to take place at seven-thirty. People were already going inside, but there were a lot more cars parked than Sophie had expected. The parish council had obviously been busy letting everyone know about the event. They stepped out of the car and Nate looked around, straightening his shoulders as though he was preparing himself for what was to come.

'There you are, Sophie! Your father said you would be here. I've been waiting for ages.' The familiar female voice startled Sophie and she looked around, her mouth opening in shock as she saw her mother standing by a bench seat that was set into the pavement.

'Mum, what are you doing here?'

Her mother looked animated, her eyes bright, her cheeks showing spots of bright colour, and her tawny, naturally curly hair was tousled as though she'd been running her fingers through it. Sophie's heart sank. Those weren't good signs. They were all indicators that her mother had been leaving off her medication.

'I wasn't expecting to see you until next weekend.'

'Well, I came to see you, of course.' She saw Nate standing beside Sophie and glared at him in recognition. 'Please go away. I want to talk to my daughter.'

Sophie looked at him in alarm, but Nate held up his hands, palms flat, and took a couple of steps backwards. He knew about her mother's condition and wasn't going to argue with her.

Her mother seemed satisfied with that for the moment. She clearly had other things on her mind. She quickly turned her attention back to Sophie and said, 'No one was at the cottage when I got here this afternoon, so I phoned your father.' She rolled her eyes. 'He wasn't any help at all. He told me to go back home. As if I would! I want to see Rob and Jessica—I thought we could all go for a picnic on the green to celebrate us being together.' She was talking fast, full of excitement about her plans.

'Mum—this isn't a good time. We're just about to go into a meeting.'

'Oh, who cares about meetings? I've a basket full of food in the car—I thought we'd spread out a cloth on the grass and enjoy ourselves.'

Sophie sucked in a swift breath. Beside her, she

felt Nate stiffen and she couldn't help worrying about what he might be thinking. It was embarrassing when her mother had these manic episodes because to her everything seemed normal and she didn't see that she was doing anything out of the ordinary.

All the times before in the past when her mother had gone off her medication came flooding back, making her stomach churn. Her mother could either go into a deep depression or feel so full of energy that she could take on the world. It was difficult to know how to deal with her sometimes. From experience, Sophie knew that any attempt to turn her mother off her goal would only end in her taking offence. Despite her seeming confidence, her illness meant she was in a highly vulnerable state.

'All right,' Sophie said, trying to talk in a soothing manner. 'Let's think about this. It's going to be dark by the time we get things sorted—so perhaps this isn't the ideal place for a picnic. How would it be if I take you back to the cottage to see Rob and Jessica? I'm sure they would love to see you and take a look at the food you've brought with you. They could help you set it out and you could have a picnic at the cottage.'

Her mother moved her head from side to side as she thought about that. 'Okay,' she said at last, and Sophie gave a silent sigh of relief.

'Good. Where's your car? Is it close by?'

'Yes, it's over there.' Her mother waved a hand towards a side street.

'Ah, I see it.' Sophie swallowed carefully, conscious all the while of time passing by and of the village hall filling up with people. She was worried about the effect this disruption must be having on Nate but he stayed silent, simply watching her with her mother, his mouth making a flat line. He was clearly disturbed by the turn of events but he wasn't going to interfere and make the situation worse. Sophie had said she would go with him to the meeting and she didn't want to let him down, but she had to take care of her mother. 'Mum, have you brought your tablets with you—are they in your bag?'

'Tablets? I hate taking them…and I don't need them. I feel great!'

'I know you do…but do you have them with you? Can I look at them?'

'Oh, this is wasting precious time.' Even so, her mother searched in her bag and triumphantly produced a bottle of capsules. 'Here, you might as well throw them away.'

Sophie took the plastic bottle and slipped it into her own bag. While her mother was preoccupied with the contents of her leather purse, she glanced at Nate and said softly, 'I'll drive her to the cottage—Rob and Jessica will look after her. It shouldn't take too long—I'll try to be back for the start of the meeting.'

'You'd better send them a message to let them know you're on your way.'

She nodded. 'I'm sorry about this.' It seemed she was always having to apologise. 'I did tell you my family is always going through problems of one sort or another.'

'Yes, you did, and I remember how it was from when you all lived here before, but it's okay. It can't be helped. I'll follow you in my car and make sure everything's all right.'

She hadn't expected him to do that. 'Are you sure? What about the meeting?'

'With any luck, we should be back in time.'

'Thanks.' She exhaled slowly. She felt better already. She turned back to her mother. 'Come on, Mum,' she said, taking her arm and leading her away. 'It's been disturbing for you lately, hasn't it, with everything that's been going on at home? But it's all working out fine.'

'Yes, it's good now. Rob and Jess are with you. They'll be all right.'

Sophie settled her mother in the car and took a moment to phone Jessica and tell her that they were on their way.

'Don't worry,' Jessica said. 'I'll make sure she takes her tablets. She'll probably sleep for a while afterwards. They often have that effect on her after she's left them off for a while.'

'Thanks.'

Back at the cottage, Jessica and Rob welcomed their mother and settled her in the recliner armchair. They started to talk to her about things that were on her mind. Over the years, they'd all found this was the best way to deal with her wild mood swings.

Satisfied that she was being well looked after, Sophie went out and slid into the passenger seat of Nate's car.

'Is she okay?'

'I think so. Rob's setting out the food and Jessica has persuaded her to take a tablet.'

'Good.' He started the car and they set off once more for the meeting.

Nate pulled up opposite the village hall. He cut the engine and looked about him, frowning. There were men and women outside the hall, holding cameras aloft, and some had recording devices. These weren't villagers.

'It's the press,' Nate said through his teeth, his mouth making a grim line. 'Who would have told them about the meeting?'

'Isn't that the chairperson from the parish council speaking to one of them?' Sophie murmured.

'He looks quite pleased with himself. I think we
can guess who told them.'

'He's gone too far this time.' Nate stepped out
of the car and went towards the gathering of people. Sophie followed him.

'There he is.' The crowd surged towards him,
cameras flashing, following him as he walked
into the hall.

'Are you selling out, Branscombe?' a reporter
shouted.

'Are you going after the money like your father?' another called out.

Nate tried to speak to the assembled people but
was cut off by another journalist. 'Sins of the father,' the man said. 'What do you say to that, eh?
Makes a good headline, don't you think?'

Nate tried to go on with what he wanted to say.
People seemed disturbed by what was going on
and Sophie caught a glimpse of her father in his
wheelchair at the side of the hall, being kept back
out of harm's way by his friend. He looked concerned by the turn of events.

'I agreed to come here this evening to talk to

all of you and try to put your minds at rest,' Nate began. He didn't get a chance to go on.

'How can you do that? Your father's landed you right in it, hasn't he?' one of the reporters interrupted.

'Yeah, how are you going to sort out his mess?' another one enquired. 'Are you going to make a mint from selling out to Peninsula?'

Nate braced his shoulders. 'Okay, that's enough,' he announced in a brisk tone. 'Either you back off or this meeting is not going ahead.'

'Peninsula Holdings are going to put this place on the map. They'll build hotels and a shopping mall. That'll all be down to you, won't it?' A man with a camera stepped up to Nate and took his picture.

Another held out his recording device. 'What do you say to the people who want to keep their village exactly as it is now?'

Nate's jaw clenched. 'That's it. I'm leaving. If the people who are villagers or tenants on the estate want to talk to me, they can come to the

Manor House tomorrow evening at seven. The press are not invited.'

He looked at Sophie. 'Are you coming with me? I'll understand if you don't want to.' He swivelled around and walked swiftly back to the car.

Sophie followed him, eyes wide, anxious about the disastrous way things had erupted and desperate to talk to him. As she turned to go, she couldn't be sure but she thought she saw Jake among the crowd. Had he gone there to take part in the meeting?

Then, as she hurried away, she caught sight of her father's expression. 'I'm sorry,' she mouthed silently. He was taut with disbelief at the way things had gone. She didn't like to dwell on what he thought of her being with the son of the man who'd caused his disability, but at that moment she felt like a traitor.

She slid into the car beside Nate and he gunned the engine into life. The journalists were blocking the road back to the cottage, so he reversed quickly, turned the car around and headed out along the main highway.

'Where are we going?' she asked.

'To the Manor House.' He shot her a quick glance. 'Is that okay with you?'

'I suppose so.' She frowned. 'I can't help thinking it would have been better if you'd stayed to talk to the villagers.'

'You're probably right, but I wasn't going to take part in a circus. I told the organisers "no press" but they didn't keep to their word.'

'They'll probably be on their way to the Manor right now,' she said quietly. 'You could be heading right into another confrontation.'

'Yes, I expect that's true. I could drive to the Wayfarer's Inn instead—it's out of the way, no one will guess we're there, and we can talk over dinner. What do you think?'

'Sounds good.'

The Wayfarer's Inn was off the beaten track along a country lane and served the residents of another small village further inland. It was set against a backdrop of tall trees and had a garden where people could sit outside at rustic tables lit by old-style lanterns. Sophie and Nate chose to go inside and found a table in a corner made private by a wooden trellis and strategically placed tubs filled with greenery.

Sophie was surprised to find she had an appetite despite the fact that she'd shared a meal with her brother and sister less than three hours ago, but Nate was making up for missing out on a proper meal earlier that day. They ate chilli con carne with pilau rice and sour cream, and finished off with apple-and-raspberry crumble. They talked about his father, who was struggling with lung problems after his heart attack.

It was only later, when Nate's mood had mellowed a little, that Sophie asked him about his plans for the estate.

'What would you have said at the meeting?' she asked him as they drank rich dark coffee. 'Do you think you would have managed to appease them?'

'Some people might have been satisfied, but others possibly not. The thing is, I don't have a lot of options. My father borrowed money to finance his investment abroad and that has to be paid back.'

She frowned. 'I can see why it's been such a worry.'

'Yes.' He made a wry face. 'I've been trying to organise ways to save the estate, but they won't be to everyone's liking. For a start, I would have to terminate short-term leases so that I can sell those properties. That would only apply to new-comers who rent property for the holiday season. We get a few people who come over from France or Spain, wanting a change of scenery. In the win-ter, the houses are difficult to let unless business people want to stay while they're over here for conferences and so on.'

He refilled his cup from a cafetière and spooned brown sugar crystals into his coffee. 'I'll see if I can start some kind of farming project, and I thought we could make more use of the lake— maybe restock it with fish and organise fishing weekends. I'm sure they would go down well.'

'You'd have to have somewhere for them to stay locally.'

He nodded. 'I could get some log cabins built by the lake...have facilities put in and so on, but it will cost quite a bit initially. I'll put my own money into that but it will be some time before the venture pays for itself.'

'So, all in all, it would have been simpler for you to sell up and have none of this problem?'

'It would. It's taken a while for the accountants to look into everything but I'm fairly sure we have some viable options now. I think I can safely turn down any offer Peninsula makes.'

She smiled. 'That's such a relief. It sounds as though you've tried really hard to find a solution.'

'I have.' He reached for her hand across the table. 'Above all, I'm doing this for you, Sophie. I told you I would do everything I can to make sure you and your father can keep your homes. I'm going down this route because I feel we—my father and I—owe it to your father to help him any way we can to make up for what happened to him, and I'm doing it because I care about you and I want you to be happy.'

'Thank you. I...I don't know what to say. I'm so grateful to you.' She leaned forward in her seat and placed her free hand in his palm. He cupped her hands and bent his head towards her, brushing her lips with his own, sending an instant wave of heat to course through her body.

'You know I want you, Sophie...more than anything. I'd move heaven and earth for you. I want to take you in my arms and kiss you right now and let you know just how much I'm aching for you.'

She kissed him, closing her eyes, oblivious to their surroundings. Her lips were aflame, her blood fizzing with excitement. Hidden by the screen, they were in their own secluded world, and in that moment she wanted him every bit as much as he wanted her.

'We could get a room here,' he said softly, his voice rough around the edges, his hands trembling a little. 'I need you so much. Tell me you feel the same way.'

'I want you,' she said huskily. 'I do...but...I'm not sure it would be the wisest thing... There are so many reasons why this would be all wrong... You and me—we're from different worlds.'

'That doesn't matter. Why should it matter?'

She thought about it. He was offering her a night

of bliss, of joy and ecstasy, the fulfilment of all her longings…but that was all he was offering. Could she put her uncertainties about everything that had happened between them and the problems between their families to one side and give in to temptation, take what he was prepared to give, for now?

Her musings were short-lived. A waiter approached and they broke apart, just as her mobile phone started to trill. Still shaken by her need for Nate, she did nothing, but took deep, slow breaths, trying to bring herself back to normal.

The phone kept on ringing. 'They're persistent, whoever they are,' Nate said drily. 'Perhaps you'd better answer it. It might be to do with your sister, or your mother.'

She nodded. The waiter asked if there was anything they needed and Nate asked for the bill. He had himself under control, as if nothing had happened between them. Either that or he was very good at hiding his feelings.

He'd had to remind her about the worries over Jessica and her mother. What had she been thinking? How could she possibly spend the night here with him when her family needed her? She couldn't leave them to their own devices so soon.

She looked down at the screen on her phone. 'It's Jake,' she said flatly. 'I thought I saw him outside the village hall earlier. He's probably worried in case the press caught up with us.'

Nate's head went back a fraction and his gaze narrowed on her. He didn't like the fact that Jake was calling her.

Jake's voice was brisk and matter-of-fact. 'I had to ring you,' he said. 'I tried to get to the Manor House in case you were there, but there are a dozen reporters at the gate. I know you're with Nate—I saw you leave the meeting with him—but I don't feel I had any choice but to get in touch. Your father's very concerned about what happened at the hall tonight. I spoke to him and he's in a bad way, very shaken up. I think he might be suffering a panic attack of some sort.'

'Thanks for letting me know, Jake. I'll go and see him.'

'I told him you would.'

'Yes…okay.'

She cut the call and told Nate what was happening. 'I'll have to go over to Dad's house and try to calm him down. You can stay here, if you want—Jake said the journalists are at the Manor. I'll get a taxi to take me home.'

He shook his head. 'I'll take you, and then I'll go to the Manor House. I'm not going to let a bunch of reporters keep me away.'

She frowned. 'So we could have gone there earlier?'

'I guess so.' He nodded. 'It's just that when you suggested there might be a problem, I thought this place might be more romantic—I suppose I leapt at the chance to spend time with you somewhere you might feel comfortable. I didn't have an ulterior motive, but I wanted you to be able to relax.'

'Hmm…and I did. You're right—this is a lovely inn.' She made a wry smile. 'And I was relaxed enough to be very tempted by your offer of spending the night, until I started to think about everything that's happened. My family has to come first. We've had more than one chance but it's just not meant to be.'

'I won't let you down again, Sophie,' he said.

'I'd like to believe that.' She stood up and he went with her towards the exit door.

'And you know I won't give up trying to win you over, don't you?'

'Mmm…I guessed as much. You always were persistent.'

He studied her as he held open the door to let her through. 'You don't believe I can be good for you, do you?'

She returned his gaze. 'No. There are so many reasons why I should steer clear of you, and an equal number of reasons why I can't—my head and my heart are at war and I've no idea what to do about that.'

He smiled. 'That's easy. Listen to your heart every time…and let me take care of the rest.'

CHAPTER SIX

'YOU WERE THERE with him at the meeting—you were there with Nate Branscombe.' Sophie's father glared at her angrily next morning. 'How could you do that? How could you ally yourself with him when you know how I feel about that family?'

'Nate's okay—he's not done anything wrong. He wasn't the one who hurt us.' Sophie tried to defend Nate but her father wasn't having any of it.

'He's in charge now and if things don't go his way he'll sell us out, plain and simple. He's a Branscombe through and through. And all this time you and he have been getting close again—I can see it in the way you look at him, in the way you talk about him... Don't fool yourself that he cares about you, Sophie. He'll do the same as he's always done with women and drop you as soon as

things start getting serious. Didn't you learn anything when he left after my accident? He didn't
stay around to help you pick up the pieces, did
he?'

'I made it too difficult for him. I was angry and
upset and I wouldn't listen. I thought someone—
he—should have known his father was having
angina attacks. I lashed out at him.'

'You weren't to blame for him leaving. He'd
have gone anyway. I worked for his father, remember? I know how his kind think. They simply move on.'

'Nate's different, Dad. He's a decent man.'

'He's messing with you. James Branscombe
always made it clear to me that his son was to
marry aristocracy. It was always uppermost in
his mind that his son would carry on the line and
keep that upper-crust heritage. His family's place
in society means everything to James. And his
son won't go against him.'

Sophie flinched at the things he was saying.
She'd probably known it all along, but having it
spelled out for her so graphically made her stom-

ach churn. Her father was upset and angry but she understood he was only trying to look out for her. He wanted to warn her there was no future for her with Nate, but deep down she already knew it, didn't she? Her problem was that she had trouble accepting it.

'I'm not looking to marry him,' she said. 'No one said anything about that.' But if she had the chance to be with Nate for ever, wouldn't she grasp it with both hands? Wasn't she lying to herself if she said anything different? But she couldn't say any of that to her father, could she? He wouldn't understand. 'Try not to upset yourself. You'll only end up having another panic attack like you did last night.' She knelt down beside her father's chair. 'Look, Dad, I'm sorry you feel this way…but I told you how Nate plans to put things right about the estate. He's doing the best he can in difficult circumstances. If you're not convinced, you'll be able to talk to him at the Manor House tonight.'

'Hmmph. We'll see.' He frowned. 'You'll be there, I suppose?'

She nodded. 'I'm going with Rob. He said he wants to know what's going on. Do you want me to take you, or will your friend be driving you there?'

'I've already made arrangements.'

'Okay.' She stood up. 'If there's nothing else I can do for you, I'd better get back to the cottage. Jessica was having some kind of cramps in her abdomen this morning. They may be nothing, but I need to take her for her check-up at the hospital.'

He nodded. 'Let me know how she goes on. Where's your mother staying? I don't suppose there's room for her at the cottage, is there? Is she any calmer?'

'She seems to be all right now. We're making sure she's taking her tablets and she's booked herself into a room at the village pub. Tom will come over when he gets the chance but it's difficult for him because he has to go to work every day and can't get away easily. Anyway, Mum says she's going to stay there until Jess has the baby. Don't worry. We'll look after her.' She laid a hand on his shoulder and bent to kiss him lightly on the forehead. 'I'll see you later, Dad. Rob will be along in an hour or so to make a start on clearing out the spare room. He's really keen to get things organised.'

She went out by the kitchen. Charlie's tail thumped happily on the floor as she stroked him before leaving the house. She'd spent a fraught half hour with her father and she was almost relieved to be going home.

Jessica was still feeling uncomfortable when Sophie arrived back at the cottage, and she did her best to reassure her. 'We'd perhaps better take your overnight case with us to the hospital,' she said. 'They might want to keep you in.'

Some half an hour later, she took her over to the maternity unit. 'Stay with me when I see the doctor, will you?' Jessica asked. 'And I want you to be there when the baby comes—I don't even know if Ryan will be able to be here for the birth. I need to have you with me.'

'That's all right. Of course I'll stay with you— and once we know that you're in labour, we can get in touch with Ryan. With any luck, he'll be able to fly home at short notice.'

'Thanks, Sophie.'

The obstetrician examined Jessica carefully and looked at the ultrasound scans. 'I think we'll admit you for observation,' she said. 'If things don't start to happen overnight, we'll induce labour in the morning.'

They found a bed for Jessica on the ward and Sophie helped her settle in. 'You can walk about if you want, use the day room and talk to the other mums-to-be,' the midwife told Jessica. 'But make sure you get some rest if you feel you need it. We'll be checking your pulse and blood pressure and listening to the foetal heartbeat and so on at regular intervals.'

'I'm leaving you in good hands,' Sophie told her sister a little later. She glanced at her watch. 'I'm here on borrowed time—I need to go over to the Children's Unit and get to work, but I'll come over to see you later.' She left Jessica making a phone call to Ryan.

The rest of the day passed without anything

untoward happening, and after checking on Jessica once more in the late afternoon, Sophie spent some time getting ready for the meeting at the Manor House. She missed Nate and wanted to be with him, but she hadn't seen much of him all day. They'd both been busy with their own lists of patients, and now she was edgy with anticipation at the thought of seeing him again at his home. Last night at the Wayfarer's Inn, he'd kissed her and made it very clear how much he wanted her. How would it have been if she'd spent the night there with him? A frisson of nervous excitement rippled through her at the thought.

A crowd of reporters had gathered outside the gates of the Manor by the time Rob and Sophie arrived, but security staff were on hand to make sure none of them had access to the grounds. They'd been told to expect Sophie and her brother, so they were allowed in without any fuss, and Sophie was able to drive up to the house without restriction.

Nate met her and Rob in the wide hallway and immediately took them to one side. 'Hey, I'm glad you came.' He greeted them cheerfully, but after a moment or two of general chit-chat, Rob excused himself and went to find his father. Nate drew Sophie into a side room.

As soon as they were alone, he put his arms around her and held her close. 'I wish there wasn't such a crowd here tonight,' he said. 'I'd much rather it was just you and me—I'd like to have the time to show you properly just how glad I am to see you.'

'That might not be such a good idea.' She felt warm and safe in his arms, but even so, she looked at him uncertainly, her father's warnings echoing in her head.

'No?' He took no notice of her doubts, folding her to him and sweeping away her qualms with a kiss that was passionate, fervent and full of pent-up desire, as though he'd been holding back and couldn't resist any longer. His kiss left her breathless, clinging to him in startled wonder, definitely wanting more.

'Oh, wow!' she said. 'I wasn't expecting that.' He held her so that her body meshed with his and she smiled up at him, loving his nearness. She was all too conscious of the way his hands were moving slowly over her, shaping her curves, exploring the soft hills and valleys of her body. It made her feel good, made her tingle all over with longing.

'I can't get enough of you,' he said, his voice ragged as he bent his head to nuzzle the silky-smooth column of her throat. He nudged aside the flimsy fabric of her top, exposing her bare shoulder. 'I've been thinking about you all night and all day, waiting until I could get you alone.' He ran the flat of his palm lightly down her spine, moving ever lower until he drew her against him and his strong thighs tangled with hers. 'You're so, so beautiful,' he whispered. 'You tantalise me every time I'm with you.'

She kissed him, a deep-seated need growing in her. She wanted this, was desperate to be with him. And yet, even as she returned his kisses and ran her fingers over his taut biceps, at the back of her mind the doubts were creeping in. Why did it have to be so difficult for her to give in to her heart's desire?

Perhaps it was because she knew, deep down, that she would never be satisfied with a relationship that was going nowhere. She wanted more, much more from Nate, but was he prepared to give it? Her whole life had been torn apart when her parents' marriage broke up, and her own relationships with men had been fraught up to now. Perhaps those experiences had made her afraid. She couldn't face being hurt again and if Nate let her down she would be devastated. More than anything, she needed to experience a love that would last—and she was coming to realise that it was *his* love she wanted above all.

She ran her hand lightly over his ribcage as though she would memorise the feel of him. She wanted him and needed him, but… When she looked up into his eyes, she knew he read the uncertainty in hers. 'I won't let you down,' he said. He kissed her passionately, his hand moving to the small of her back, crushing her soft curves to blend with his.

A clock chimed the hour and he sighed, releasing her slowly. 'We should go,' he murmured reluctantly, resting his head lightly against her temple, and she nodded. 'I didn't want any of this,' he said quietly. 'This business of the Manor and the estate. I simply wanted to be a doctor.'

They broke apart and she spent a moment tidying herself up, straightening her camisole top and smoothing a hand over her jeans. 'Is my hair a mess?' she asked and he gave her an amused smile.

'You look fantastic,' he said. 'You always do. That's part of the problem.' There was a faint note of regret in his voice.

They went into the main hall, where people were beginning to take their places around a long, rectangular solid wood table, and Sophie slid into a seat next to her brother and her father. The walls in here were panelled in oak and the evening light filtered in through leaded panes, casting a warm glow over everything.

Nate welcomed everyone. He'd provided them with tea and coffee and soft drinks or wine, and there was a buffet table at the side of the room behind Sophie, where a selection of finger food had been set out. Sophie guessed that his house-keeper, Charlotte, had been busy organising things. She noticed that as well as a variety of tiny sandwiches, there were mini Yorkshire puddings with rare beef and mustard and horseradish sauce, bruschetta with goat's cheese, basil and tomato, and blinis with smoked salmon. He'd done his best to make sure his guests were treated well.

His efforts certainly helped to put his audience in a better mood and encourage them to listen to what he had to say. He told them of the plans he'd outlined to Sophie, and added that he was hoping to start an organic farming business on the land that up to now had been left to pasture. 'I'll need skilled workers to help me with that,' he said.

There were some dissenting voices. Some people didn't like the fact that he was planning to organise fishing weekends. 'There'll be a lot of strangers roaming around, and they'll start up competitions and so on,' one man said. 'The village won't be the same.'

'It's better than having to sell the houses to Peninsula, though, don't you think?' Nate pointed out the advantages but added, 'The costings aren't all in yet, so I'm making no promises…but this is what I'm aiming for. I'll do my best to hold off any sale.'

When the meeting finished, people stayed to eat some more and talk for a while and ask questions but gradually they started to drift away. Sophie's father spoke to her briefly. He seemed slightly appeased by what he'd heard but said tetchily, 'I'm going home. I can't be in this place without remembering all my dealings with James Branscombe. He was a difficult man to work with. I don't know if his son's going to be different— let's hope he is.'

Rob frowned, watching his father leave. 'He's very bitter still, isn't he? I can't blame him. His whole life changed after the accident. I just don't know why he stayed with Lord Branscombe so long if he felt that way about him.'

'I think the money was probably good, and the

work suited him. It kept a roof over our heads. People put up with a lot to have a secure life.'

'Perhaps he'll feel better when I go to live with him. I'll be able to help him out if he's struggling.'

'That's true.' Sophie nodded. 'Though sometimes it might do him good to struggle a bit.'

Rob frowned. 'How can that be?'

'It might help him to do things for himself as much as possible.'

'But he can't, can he? He's in a wheelchair.'

Nate came to join them. 'I couldn't help overhearing the last bit of your conversation,' he said. 'I think Sophie means that if your father has to try to do some things within his ability, it will help strengthen his muscles. Being able to pull himself up to a standing position, for instance, will help—though he'll need someone to be there with him to make sure he doesn't fall.'

'Oh, I see.' Rob nodded thoughtfully. 'Yes, I can do that.'

Nate studied him. 'How are you doing these days, Rob? Are you feeling any brighter in yourself?'

Rob pulled a face. 'I think I'm better now I'm a bit more settled. I have mood swings and I don't understand why I feel that way. I worry about it sometimes.'

'That's understandable.' Nate was sympathetic. 'Sophie told me you were afraid you might be suffering from bipolar disorder like your mother but, to be honest, seeing you and hearing how you react to things, I think you're going through what every teenage boy goes through. Your hormones are all over the place. It's a difficult time for you.'

'I think Nate's right.' Sophie joined in. She was glad Nate had taken the time to try to reassure her brother. 'You've been better in yourself since you came here and met up with some of your old friends. You said a few of them are studying at the college in town—perhaps you might want to look into signing up for one of the courses that start soon. You've already done a year of Psychology—why not try to finish your studies?'

Rob gave it some thought and then nodded, seemingly invigorated. 'Yeah, I might do that.

My mate has to go to an Open Day in a couple of weeks. I could go along with him.'

'That's a great idea.'

Nate glanced at Sophie. 'How's the rest of the family doing?'

'They're fine, thanks.' He already knew about Jessica being admitted to hospital. 'Jess's still having odd abdominal cramps—they're not really contractions as such but she's quite uncomfortable. Her back's aching and she doesn't like being on her own in hospital. And I checked on Mum before we came here and made sure she took her tablets.' She sent him a quick concerned glance. 'Is there any news of your father?'

'He's much the same. He's been readmitted to hospital so he can have intensive treatment. They have him on antibiotics and diuretics to try to reduce the fluid in his tissues, but he seems to be struggling.'

'I'm sorry.'

She and Rob had to go soon after that so that Sophie could drive to the hospital and check on Jessica. She was reluctant to leave Nate—she wanted to stay and talk some more—but her sister was uppermost in her mind just then.

Jessica was thrilled to see her and Rob. They spoke for a short time and Sophie rubbed her back for her, but Jess was tired and soon dozed off. It looked as though they would go ahead with inducing labour in the morning.

Everything went as planned. A whole day went by after the midwife inserted the pessary that would hopefully start things off. By then the weekend was almost on them and Sophie was glad because it meant she would be able to spend time at the hospital without worrying about having to take time off work.

She went to the village High Street on Saturday morning to buy things that Jessica might need, like baby bottles, nappies and wipes. She found a lovely congratulations card and some of Jessica's favourite chocolates. Lost in thought, she came back out on to the street only to be pulled up short in surprise as she saw Nate coming out of the post office. Her pulse quickened.

'Hi there. It's good to see you.' He smiled and gave her a hug. 'I wasn't sure if I would see anything of you over the next couple of days, with Jessica being in hospital, but here you are. It's my lucky day.' He waved a hand towards the post office. 'I had to send off a registered letter—' He glanced at her packages. 'It looks as though you've been stocking up on essentials in preparation for the baby.'

She nodded. 'Jessica brought a few things with her on the train, but there was a limit to what she could get in her case. As it was, it was a good thing it had wheels on it.' They walked along the street together to where she had parked her car.

'Are you headed for the hospital now?'

'Yes, I—' She broke off, frowning as she noticed a small boy walking with his mother. They were going towards the pharmacy nearby and the child was coughing quite badly, dragging his feet as though being out and about was too much for him. He was a thin little boy around seven years old and he was breathless and didn't look at all well. His mother looked at him worriedly, supporting him, and as Sophie and Nate looked on, the little boy's knees started to buckle under him.

Nate reached them and helped to catch the child before he collapsed completely. 'Can I help you?' he asked the mother. 'He looks quite poorly.' He held the child, kneeling down and cradling him in his arms as his mother nodded anxiously.

'Oh, yes...please can you help?' She knelt down beside him, saying urgently, 'I recognise you— you're Nate Branscombe, aren't you? Can you do something for him? You're a doctor, aren't you? I tried to get to see our GP but the surgery's closed.'

She dragged in a shaky breath. 'My little boy's had a cough for about a week but the antibiotics the doctor gave him don't seem to be working. I'm on my own this weekend. I've been so worried. I'm new to the village and I have no transport and no one I can leave him with while I try to sort out what to do. I was going to the pharmacy to see if anyone could help, but he suddenly got worse. I knew he was ill but I didn't think it was so bad—I think I need to call for an ambulance.'

'Yes, that would probably be best,' Nate said.

He glanced up at Sophie but she was already dialling the number. 'He's feverish and not breathing properly,' Nate went on. 'He needs oxygen.' He looked at Sophie once more. 'Do you have your medical kit in your car? I have mine but I'm parked further down the road.' He checked the boy over, feeling for a pulse. 'His lips are a bluish colour already. I'm afraid we may need to intubate him fast.'

'Yes, I'll go and get it.' Finishing the call, she hurriedly opened the boot of her car and hauled out her copious medical bag. Taking off her jacket, she rolled it up into the shape of a pillow and placed it under the boy's head. She placed an SpO2 monitor on his finger and connected it to the portable machine that gave an oxygen read-out.

'What's his name?' Nate asked the mother.

'Shaun.'

'Okay.' He spoke directly to the boy. 'Shaun, I'm going to listen to your chest.' The boy didn't respond but Nate reached for a stethoscope and was quiet for a moment, running the diaphragm over Shaun's ribcage. 'It sounds like pneumonia,' he said after a while. He checked the SpO2 reading. 'His blood oxygen saturation is very low,' he told Sophie. 'The most important thing right now is to get a tube into his windpipe and give him the oxygen he needs.'

Sophie helped him, introducing a cannula into Shaun's hand and giving him a sedative and anaesthetic so that Nate could get easier access to insert the tube into his throat. They worked quickly, taping the tube in place on the boy's cheek. Nate connected the tube to the bag and mask device and then attached this to an oxygen canister. He began to squeeze the bag rhythmically, getting life-saving oxygen into Shaun's lungs.

Sophie explained the procedure to the mother and then said, 'When he gets to the hospital he'll most likely be given an X-ray and possibly a CT scan to take a better look at his lungs. They'll want to do tests to see what's causing the problem and they'll give him a stronger broad spectrum antibiotic in the meantime.'

In the distance, they heard the sound of the ambulance siren. Nate looked up, frowning slightly as he saw that a crowd of onlookers had gathered around them. They were mostly silent, just watching, but Nate was too busy to take much notice. 'I'm going to give him nebulised adrenaline,' he told Sophie. 'Will you take over here while I set it up?'

'Of course.' She squeezed the oxygen bag while he prepared the nebulised solution. It would help to relax the child's airways and allow him to breathe more easily. After a while, when the boy was still unresponsive, he gave him a shot of corticosteroid, aiming to reduce any inflammation that was causing a problem. Sophie went on squeezing the oxygen bag and Nate spoke quietly to the child's mother, trying to reassure her.

The ambulance drew up close by. 'Hi, Doc—hi, Sophie...' The paramedics arrived and listened carefully as Nate outlined the situation.

'We need to have a team waiting for us at the hospital. He should go straight to Paediatric Intensive Care.'

'Okay, we'll let them know.'

They transferred Shaun to the ambulance and connected him to the monitors that would tell them his heart and respiratory rate, along with the level of oxygen in his blood. It was improving but it was still very low because of the infection in his lungs. Shaun's mother sat alongside her son and Nate climbed into the vehicle to make the journey with them.

He glanced at Sophie. 'Thanks for everything you did back there, Sophie. Maybe I'll see you at the hospital later?' He was looking at her packages, abandoned on the pavement.

She nodded. 'Yes, I'll be there most of the day, I expect.' She watched the ambulance pull away and then went to gather up all her equipment.

The small crowd of people were still watching. 'You and the other doctor did all right, there,' one man said. 'Do you think the boy will pull through?'

'Well, we've done everything we can and he'll be in the right place to get the care he needs,' she answered carefully.

'I never thought of Nate Branscombe working as an emergency doctor,' another bystander said. 'I only ever saw him coming and going from the Manor House.' He nodded slowly, deep in thought. 'Just goes to show, you never really know someone.'

Sophie collected her supplies and put them back into her medical bag. She stowed it away in the boot of her car, along with her shopping. A woman who Sophie recognised from around the village picked up one of the bags from the pavement and handed it to her. 'Baby things,' she said with a smile. 'I guessed your sister would be due any time now. I hope things go well for her.'

'Thanks.' Sophie smiled and slid into the driver's seat. She and Nate had spent a worrying half hour or so with the boy and she was almost looking forward to enjoying a more relaxed time in the maternity unit with Jessica.

Perhaps she ought to have known it wasn't to be. Life was never that easy for her, and when she arrived on the ward Jessica was nowhere to be seen.

'Oh, she's been taken to the delivery suite,' a

nurse told her. 'She's not doing too well, poor girl. The contractions have been painful and they've been going on for quite a long time through the night. The doctor's given her an epidural to give her some relief.'

'But she didn't tell me… Why wouldn't she have phoned me?'

'She said if it was going to be a long haul she didn't want to worry you. I was about to call you, though. Things are beginning to speed up quite significantly.'

'I'll go and see her.'

Sophie hurried away to find Jessica. She was lying on the bed looking very pale, with a sheen of sweat on her brow. 'Oh, Jessica, you were supposed to ring me,' Sophie said, going over to her to give her a hug. 'Did you change your mind about wanting me here?'

'No! Never!' Jessica smiled tiredly. 'It's just that it all started to happen in the night and I guessed you'd be asleep. I didn't want to disturb you. And Mum was here earlier. She can be a bit exhausting when she's in full flow. I'm not sure she's taken her tablets.'

'Oh, heavens! Where is she now?'

'She's gone to get a cup of coffee. Do you think you might be able to persuade her to swallow her meds with a bun or something?'

'I will...but shouldn't I be here with you?'

'You will be. They say it will be a while yet.' Jessica smiled, laying a hand on her abdomen as another contraction swept over her. 'I can feel it but since I had the epidural there's no pain. I'll be fine. I think Ryan's on his way to the hospital. He said he was going to catch a flight last night.'

'That's good. All right, I'll go and see if I can find Mum and calm her down—though I suppose you can't really blame her for being excited with a grandson on the way!'

Jessica smiled. 'Yes, maybe.'

Sophie found her mother in the cafeteria, happily sending messages from her phone to all her friends. 'I can't believe it's actually happening,' she said. 'But she's been in labour for ages.'

'It's taking a while, isn't it?' Sophie agreed. 'But

a first grandchild is something special...worth waiting for.'

'Oh, I can't wait to hold him!'

'I know. I feel the same way.'

They chatted and she persuaded her mother to eat something and swallow her tablets. Tom phoned a little later and Sophie took the opportunity to slip away while her mother was preoccupied with the call. 'I'll see you in a little while,' she mouthed as she left the cafeteria and her mother smiled.

She went back into the delivery room and saw, to her relief, that Ryan had arrived. He was holding Jessica's hand.

She and Ryan greeted one another and then Sophie went to stand at the other side of the bed. 'I'm so glad you made it in time,' she told him. But, even as she said it, things started to happen all at once. Another major contraction started.

'I can see the baby's head,' the midwife said. 'Try to give a big push.'

The baby's head appeared, but instead of being followed by the appearance of his shoulders, ev-

224 SECOND CHANCE WITH LORD BRANSCOMBE

erything seemed to stop. They waited for Jessica's next contraction, but even then the baby's shoulders stayed firmly in place and when the midwife intervened it was no use.

'The shoulder's stuck,' she said, looking worried. The baby's face was turning grey and Sophie was becoming more alarmed with every minute that passed. If the baby stayed in this position for too long, the umbilical cord would be squashed and oxygen wouldn't get through to him.

The midwife had signalled for help and the room filled with people: obstetricians, paediatricians, midwives, an anaesthetist. They all had a specific job to do but seeing them all there, trying to bring this baby into the world, was terrifying. As a doctor, Sophie knew the dangers but this was different—this was her sister at risk, along with her unborn baby.

Two midwives helped Jessica to get into a better knees-up position to facilitate the birth, the doctor made a deeper episiotomy cut and another midwife pressed down hard on Jessica's abdomen. The baby was in distress and Jessica began to haemorrhage. It was horrifying to stand there and see it happen, and for Sophie to know that she had to keep out of the way and let the doctors and nurses do their jobs. This was her sister and her nephew who were in danger and she was frightened for both of them.

In the next minute the baby was born, but he didn't make any sound. He was a bluish colour and floppy, and immediately the paediatrician took him and began to try to resuscitate him. A midwife wrapped him in a blanket to keep him warm and then the doctor suctioned him to clear away the secretions that were blocking his airway. They placed him in an incubator and started to give him oxygen, attaching vital monitor leads to him before wheeling him away to the Neonatal Intensive Care Unit.

Sophie wanted to rush after him and do anything she could to help, but her sister needed her too. Ryan was white with shock and looked about ready to pass out, while Jessica was clammy with exhaustion and loss of blood. She was still bleeding and the midwives were doing everything they could to stem the flow. Sophie tried to stay calm, urging Ryan to sit down and put his head between his knees for a while to restore his blood pressure, and then she went to hold Jessica's hand once more.

Over the next hour, as the doctors and the nurses did everything they could to bring the bleeding under control, Jessica kept vomiting. All Sophie and Ryan could do was to try to make her comfortable. Sophie spoke to her mother and tried to reassure her—they'd been allowed to take it in turns to be in the delivery room.

'I believe things have calmed down finally,' the doctor said at last. 'She's stable, and the best thing to do now is to let her rest.'

Sophie and her mother left Jessica alone with Ryan from time to time over the next couple of hours, to give them some space. Her mother went to fetch coffees for everyone and Sophie went outside for a breath of fresh air.

Her phone rang. It was Nate, and relief washed over her at the sound of his voice. Everything seemed better when he was close by, even if he was only at the end of a phone line.

'I wondered how things were going,' he asked. 'I've been thinking about all of you.'

'She's had a really tough time and I'm worried about the baby,' she told him. 'I don't know exactly how he's doing, yet, but I think he's out of the woods. Jessica's still retching. They're giving her oxygen through nasal tubes and she's on intravenous fluids, so she's gradually improving.'

'I'm sorry, Sophie. It sounds as though it's been rough on her and the baby. Are you going to stay there through the night?'

'No, Ryan's the only one who can be with her then. The rest of the time they're not allowing more than two visitors at the bedside and Mum's going to be there for a while. Actually, I was almost expecting her to be overexcited despite her medication, but she's been remarkably subdued.'

'She's probably worried, like everyone else. I guess when she takes her medication she's fine.'

'Yes.' She frowned. 'I'm glad you understand, Nate.' Somehow, it was becoming more and more important to her that he accepted her family as they were. 'I was afraid you might be uncomfortable around my family. They can be difficult to handle at times.'

He gave a short laugh. 'I'm hardly likely to feel that way—there are skeletons in most family backgrounds, mine included, and my father isn't exactly a prime example of how to behave.'

'I suppose not.' She wished he could be here with her right now. She yearned for his soothing presence but it wasn't to be. He was probably going to spend time with his father.

Sophie cut the call a little later, after telling him, 'I'll stay with Jessica for another couple of hours and then I'm going to see Dad and Rob and let them know what's happening. After that I'm going home. It's been a traumatic day.'

Before going back to Maternity, Sophie looked in on the Children's Unit and checked up on Shaun to see how he was getting on. He'd been in a bad way when the ambulance brought him to the hospital earlier that morning and she was worried about his condition.

'He's on powerful antibiotics,' Tracey told her. 'He'll stay on the ventilator for some time, but he seems to be responding to the treatment.'

'That's something, anyway,' Sophie said. 'Thanks, Tracey.' She checked on Josh, the five-year-old who had the head injury, but he was doing fine. He was almost well enough to be discharged home.

She went to see her sister one more time. Her mother was keeping her company, concerned for her youngest daughter and holding her hand.

'I feel so dizzy,' Jessica murmured, glancing at Sophie. 'The baby—is he all right? I wish he was here. Have you been to look at him? Ryan's gone to see him.'

'Yes, I looked in on him in the Neonatal Unit,' Sophie told her. 'They're keeping him warm and giving him oxygen. When you're a little stronger and the baby's more up to it, you'll be able to hold him.'

'I wish I didn't feel so tired,' Jessica said. 'I feel so weak—the room's spinning.'

Sophie gently squeezed her hand. 'It's because

you haemorrhaged—you're very short on iron, so they're going to give you a transfusion. You should start to feel much better after that.'

Sophie's mother left to go and meet her husband and tell him what had been happening, but Jessica asked Sophie to stay. 'I feel better having you and Ryan with me,' she said.

Jessica had the blood transfusion soon after that, and an hour later Ryan wheeled the baby into the side room where she was recovering. The baby was a much healthier colour now and looked none the worse for his ordeal. He was well wrapped up in a shawl and had a soft wool hat on his head to keep him warm.

Ryan carefully laid the baby on Jessica's chest and she wrapped an arm around the sleeping infant. 'We're going to call him Casey,' she said with a smile, and her husband kissed her tenderly. She was still very weak, but the three of them were together at last and Sophie breathed a sigh of relief, watching them. It looked as though mother and son were out of danger. She took some photos for posterity and then slipped out of the room to give them some privacy.

She went to see her father and tell him about the new addition to the family. Rob was with him, getting the spare room ready while they waited for news, and he and her father were both glad to hear that disaster had been avoided. 'I think the baby is a bit jaundiced,' she told them, 'so the medical team might have to deal with that, as well as making sure that Jessica recovers her strength.'

'Maybe we could go and see her if she's going to be staying in hospital for a few days,' her father said and Sophie nodded.

'Yes, I'll take both of you. Ryan's going to stay with her until they let her come home and then she'll come back to live with me for a while, until he finishes this project he's working on. As soon as that's done, he's going to take paternity leave to be with her and the baby.'

'I'm glad he made it back here in time.' Rob was proud to be an uncle and pored over the photos with his father.

She left them a little later and went home. It

was late evening by then and she realised she had missed out on a meal. Her stomach was rumbling and she set about making a quick broccoli, pasta and cheese bake.

The doorbell rang as she set the table and she wondered if Rob had forgotten his key.

'Hi, Sophie.' Nate stood outside her front door, looking wonderful, his dark eyes glittering as he gazed at her in the evening light, his body honed and full of vitality. He was wearing smart casuals, chinos and a dark shirt.

'Come in.' She smiled at him and showed him along the hallway to the kitchen. 'I wasn't expecting you, but you must have smelled the food. There's plenty. Would you like to eat with me?'

'Mmm…smells good. It'll have to be a quick bite, though,' he said regretfully. 'I've been with my father most of the day and I need to go back to the hospital in a while.'

She frowned. 'It's bad, then?'

He nodded. 'I came away for a while so that the nurses could tend to him. I thought I'd check up on you—see how you're bearing up. I guessed you'd be back by now.' He folded her into his arms. 'I've been thinking about you all day, wondering how you were getting on, missing you.'

'I'm fine—we're all doing great after all the worry.'

'I'm glad about that.' He kissed her tenderly, holding her close and making her body surge with heat.

She kissed him, loving the way his hand rested on the swell of her hip, until all at once there was a loud beeping sound that erupted on the airwaves and destroyed the moment.

'Oh...it's the oven timer,' she said in dismay. 'My broccoli bake is ready to serve.'

He laughed. 'We'd better go and see to it, then, before it spoils.'

'Okay.' She pulled herself together and fetched hot plates from the oven and served out the food. 'Sit down. Help yourself to extra cheese and there's hot crusty bread and a green salad to go with it, if you want.'

He sat across the table from her and began

to eat. 'Mmm…it's delicious,' he said, and she smiled.

'Rob and Jessica like this—it's one of their favourite meals. They always ask for it when they come to visit.'

He studied her thoughtfully. 'You've always looked after them, haven't you? I suppose with your mother's condition affecting her so badly in those first few years they turned to you?'

'Pretty much, yes. Sometimes Mum would go off for days at a time, so we had to manage as best we could. I felt so guilty when I left to go to Medical School. I came home whenever I could—most weekends and sometimes in the week if my shifts allowed for it. And of course I spent my holidays with them. They were still so young and things were topsy-turvy for them.'

'But now things seem to be turning out all right—Rob is back with your father and planning on going to college, and Jessica is a mother herself.' He speared a forkful of salad and glanced at her. 'That must seem strange to you—it's happened so soon, while she's still so very young. Do you ever think of having a family of your own?'

She nodded. 'One day, yes, I'd like that. I hope it will happen. Seeing Jess's baby has made me feel even more maternal. He's so soft and warm and beautiful.' She drew in a deep, happy breath. 'They let me hold him and it's the best feeling in the world.' He smiled and she said quietly, 'What about you, Nate? Have you thought what it might be like to have your own babies up at the Manor House?'

He was still for a moment, his fork poised in mid-air. Then he let it settle once more on his plate and flicked a glance over her, his gaze searching, intent. 'I've thought about it,' he said at last. 'Sometimes, especially of late, I wonder what it would be like. I'm not sure, though. It's becoming more difficult for me to contemplate as time goes on.'

She studied him cautiously. 'Because you haven't found the right woman or because you don't want to deal with that aristocratic heritage and all that goes along with it?'

'It's neither of those things, really. I suppose, in my heart of hearts, I'm afraid to open up to any woman. It's only happening now because of you, I think. I never understood it before, but of late I've been thinking things through, trying to sort out my feelings. I don't feel I can trust things to work out right. I think the way I am has a lot to do with my mother dying when I was so very young... When you have that wonderful relationship with your mother, you have a right to expect it to last for ever, and as a child I was shocked to the core when it was taken from me.'

'You didn't ever get over it?'

He shrugged. 'You do, of course—not get over it, exactly, but you learn to adjust. There was a void in my life. But then, after a while, my father started to bring girlfriends back to the Manor... He was determined never to marry again—no one could replace my mother in his eyes, I think... but those relationships would last at most two, three years, maybe, and during that time I grew attached to a couple of the girls. They were decent women and I think they meant well—they were each affectionate and sweet towards me and I liked having them around, being able to confide in them…but then the relationship with my father would come to an end and they would disappear back where they came from and I never saw them again. I felt…empty…and lost.'

He shook his head, deep in thought. 'Bringing children into the world is a huge responsibility. They need stability but I don't know what it's like to have a lasting, loving relationship and I'm almost afraid that for me it doesn't exist. The experience has left me feeling that I can't risk putting all my faith in one woman. I tend to think that, somehow or other, I'll always be let down.'

'So it's best not to care too much in the first place?' She gave him a regretful, sympathetic look. 'That's a sad way to go through life but I understand how you feel. I have the same fears sometimes. Maybe we should both try to be braver and learn to take a bit of a risk in our lives.'

He gave her a wistful smile. 'Maybe.' His eyes darkened. 'I'm beginning to realise there's only one woman who could persuade me to take a chance on love…and that's you, Sophie. You mean more to me than I can put into words. I couldn't bear to lose you but I… After what my father put your family through, I'm not sure I deserve you.'

Sophie's eyes widened at the revelation. It wasn't exactly a declaration of love but it was probably as near as he'd ever come to it. 'You mustn't think that way,' she said. Her heart burned with longing. Would he one day be able to tell her what she wanted to hear—that he loved her every bit as much as she loved him?

'I wish—' He might have been about to say more but his phone began to trill and he looked down at the screen and read the text message there. 'It's my father,' he said. 'The doctor thinks I should go to see him. It sounds urgent.'

'I'm sorry.'

He stood up. 'Thanks for the meal, Sophie. I'm glad Jessica and the baby are all right.'

She went with him to the door and opened it to let him into the night. She didn't want him to go but knew that he had no choice. Then, as he walked away from her along the path, she saw to her dismay that Jake was heading towards her. The two men crossed by each other on the path and she saw Nate look at Jake and frown before nodding to him and going on his way. What must he be thinking?

It was more than likely he would be disturbed and concerned, jealous, even, but after what he'd just said to her, would he ever be persuaded that he could trust in her love? Could she ever hope to have a future with him?

'Sophie,' Jake said, coming over to her. 'I hope you don't mind me dropping in like this. I bought a present for Jessica's baby—and some course notes for Rob. He was asking me about working in a hospital and what kind of courses he should follow.'

'That's brilliant, Jake. Thanks.' She gave an inward sigh and braced herself. 'Come in.'

CHAPTER SEVEN

'DO YOU THINK Casey's skin's a better colour now, Sophie?' In her room in the Maternity Unit Jessica held her baby close to her, unwrapping his shawl and lifting his vest to show his chest. 'He was so yellow before with the jaundice but I think the treatment's working, don't you?'

Sophie smiled. 'Oh, yes…he looks much better now.' He was a beautiful baby, with a sweet rosebud mouth and perfect little fingers that curled into fists.

Jessica looked relieved. She wrapped the baby up warmly and held him against her. 'I've been so worried. The last thing you want is for your baby to have to stay in hospital for treatment when he's so tiny. Poor little man—having to have his eyes covered while he's under the special lamp for two or three hours at a time.'

'I would think he only needs a few more hours of phototherapy and then his levels of bilirubin will be back to normal,' Sophie said. 'I know it's been difficult but he's slept through it for the most part, so I don't think it's bothered him too much.'

The midwife had explained the problem of jaundice to Jessica but as a new young mother she was understandably worried. Quite often in newborn babies it was possible that the liver didn't work all that efficiently for the first couple of weeks, so the level of bilirubin could build up in the blood. Usually, it cleared up on its own, but if that didn't happen the baby could be given phototherapy. The light used in this treatment helped to change the bilirubin to a form that could be more easily broken down by the liver.

'I'm so glad you and Ryan have been able to be here with me,' Jessica said. 'It's made everything so much better. I know you have to work, but it's been good having you come in several times a day to see us. And Mum will be coming again at the weekend. It's all worked out far better than I expected.'

'Of course it has. And I have everything waiting for you back at home when you're ready to be discharged.'

Her day's work had ended some time ago and Sophie left her sister and the baby a little later, to go back to the cottage once more. If only the rest of her worries could be so easily resolved.

She was anxious for Nate. While she and her family had celebrated a wonderful new addition to the family, his own situation had become tragic. His father's health had steadily deteriorated and a few days ago Nate had broken the bad news to her that his father had passed away.

'He had another heart attack,' he'd said flatly. 'I have a lot of things to deal with, so I probably won't be able to see you for a while. I'm going to take a few days off work to make the funeral arrangements, and I have to get in touch with all my relatives. They're scattered far and wide over the country, so I expect a good many of them will want to come and stay at the Manor for a while.'

'Are you coping all right? Is there anything I can do?' Sophie asked, but he'd been determined to manage by himself. She wanted to be with him but he'd shut himself away to grieve alone. Sophie's only consolation was that Charlotte was with him and would do her best to comfort him and steer him through this difficult time.

Back at the cottage Sophie prepared for the funeral that was being held next day. Nate had said he hoped she would be there. She'd picked out a black suit with a fitted jacket and a pencil-line skirt that she felt would be suitable for the occasion. Teamed with a grey silk blouse and black stiletto heels, she felt the outfit would give her a bit more confidence.

Her father had received a formal invitation too, because he had been for a long time a trusted worker on Lord Branscombe's estate. He showed the beautifully embossed card to Sophie. 'It came with a letter too,' he said. 'I suppose that was thoughtful of Nate Branscombe—that personal touch—knowing how I felt about his father.'

'Will you go to the service?' Sophie had asked.

To her surprise, he nodded. 'Rob said he'll take me. I thought about it long and hard before

I made the decision. I've been bitter and resentful for such a long time, feeling that I was treated badly. All along, I blamed James for insisting I went on that flight with him, for not listening to reason when people told him he shouldn't pilot the plane while he was feeling unwell...but the truth is, I should have refused to go with him. It was my own weakness in not standing up to him that led to me being in the position I'm in now. I only have myself to blame.'

'Oh, Dad...' Sophie's voice broke in a sob as she knelt down beside her father's wheelchair. 'You're not to blame for anything,' she protested, laying a hand on his arm. 'I think most people would have accepted his word for it that he felt he was up to it. He was your boss and in the end you went along with what he said because ultimately you trusted him to do the right thing.'

She gently squeezed his arm, wanting to show her support. 'You always did everything you thought was for the best...and you've worked so hard to try to walk again; you've been so stoical this last couple of years. I'm proud of the way you've pushed yourself. And you're getting there… It's taking a while but you *will* walk again. Rob's told me how hard you've been working with him at your physio. You're making progress all the while. Please don't blame yourself for any of this.'

He patted her hand. 'You're a sweet girl. You've always been there for me. I'm sorry I've given you such a hard time these last few weeks over James's son. I suppose I've been harsh in judging Nate. None of this is his fault.'

She looked at him in surprise. 'Are you telling me you've changed your mind about him?'

He shrugged awkwardly. 'Let's say I'm reserving my opinion of him. I heard the talk in the village about how you and he saved that little boy—the one who collapsed and couldn't breathe. I know the child's still in hospital but he's a lot better, isn't he? It made me think about Nate in a different way. And then I heard he got in touch with the mother's family to make sure she had some support. Apparently her cousin has come over here to stay with her. They were good friends before they eventually lost touch with one another,' the woman said.'

Sophie's eyes widened. 'I hadn't heard that—Nate didn't say anything to me about it.'

'Ah, well, the boy's mother's been chatting in the post office.' He smiled. 'You know how word gets around.'

She nodded. 'I do.' It made her feel warm inside to know that Nate had done what he could to help the boy's mother.

The weather blessed them on the day of the funeral. Summer was drifting into autumn and the leaves on the trees were turning to red and gold. There was a faint breeze blowing but the sun put in an appearance through puffy white clouds so that the mourners could gather in peace. The service and the rest of the proceedings went without a hitch.

Nate was immaculately dressed, surrounded by a host of relatives Sophie had never met before. He introduced her to them but the names soon became a blur. She smiled politely and made sympathetic comments and hoped that she was being of some help to Nate by being there alongside him.

'I hadn't expected so many people from the village to turn up,' he commented as they ate canapés at the reception afterwards.

'No, nor did I.' She made a slight smile. 'But I think your standing in the village has gone up lately, since you helped young Shaun…and since you outlined your plans to save the estate.'

'Hmm…I only hope I'll be able to live up to what I said back then.' He was frowning and she looked at him curiously.

'Is there a problem?'

'I think there might be but I'm not sure how much of a setback it's going to be. My father's solicitor wants an urgent meeting with me. All I can say is that from the initial conversation I've had with him, the situation doesn't sound promising.'

She sucked in a quick breath. 'Will you let me know if things change?'

'Of course.' He was solemn but his expression became taut all at once, and when she followed the line of his gaze, she saw he was looking directly at Jake. Jake was there as a mutual friend but it seemed Nate didn't want to speak to him just then. 'I'll leave you two alone together,' he said, excusing himself and moving away from her as Jake came towards them. 'I should go and talk to some of my relatives.'

'But Jake will be wanting to speak to you,' she protested. 'He'll want to offer his condolences.'

He shook his head. 'I don't think so. He's looking at you, Sophie. He's been looking at you for the last half hour. Besides, I ought to circulate a bit.'

Jake had been watching her? She was startled Nate had noticed something to which she'd been totally oblivious, but it was clear he wasn't intending to stay around. Nate left her and went to speak to an uncle who had taken up a position by the buffet table.

Sophie exhaled slowly and greeted Jake with a slight nod of her head. 'Hi, Jake. I'm sorry we have to meet again on an occasion like this.'

'Yes, me too.' Jake studied her. 'I hope you

know what you're doing with Nate. He let you down before and he'll quite likely do it again.'

'He didn't let me down. I think he went away because he had to come to terms with what his father had done and he couldn't bear to see the pain it caused our family. He tried to talk to me about it but I wasn't ready to listen back then.'

She laid a hand on his arm. 'Thank you for looking out for me. You've always been a great friend to me,' she said quietly. 'One I'll always treasure.'

'Likewise.'

She smiled. 'Have you heard any more from Cheryl?'

He shook his head. 'A couple of emails. That's all.'

'Hmm. I think you were wrong about her wanting someone else. I happen to know that she's very keen to meet up with you again.' She lifted her brows. 'I heard she was desperately hoping you might want to take her to the annual get-together next month.'

He laughed. 'You're joking with me! How would you hear something like that?'

'The hospital grapevine, you know? She confided in a friend, who told another friend, who spilled the beans to someone who works in Accounts.'

A faint smile curved his mouth. Sophie knew she had set him thinking about a particular course of action but she said no more about it. Instead, she let her glance wander across the room to where Nate was standing. He was looking at her intently, frowning, but when she caught his gaze he turned away and spoke to his companion. He didn't look at all happy, seeing her with Jake. Perhaps he'd misinterpreted their smiles and gestures. No matter what she'd told him to the contrary, he clearly believed she and Jake were an item.

She didn't see Nate again for a few days. When she tried phoning him, he was too busy to say much and she was left feeling dissatisfied and unhappy. She desperately wanted to be with him, to be able to comfort him, but it seemed he simply wanted to be left alone.

He went to London to meet with his father's solicitor and to have further talks with Peninsula. He hadn't told Sophie what the talks were about, except to say that he wanted to clarify things after his father's passing...but when she walked Charlie by the Manor one day and saw valuable paintings being loaded on to a prominent art dealer's van, she guessed something was very wrong. This was a legitimate fine-art dealer from London. Selling the paintings had never been part of Nate's plan to recover the estate.

Whatever the outcome of those appointments in London, Sophie was shocked, along with everyone else in the village, when Peninsula announced just a few days later that they were holding a meeting in the village hall on Saturday afternoon. 'We want to discuss possibilities for the area,' their spokesman said. 'Come along and listen to what we have to say.'

Sophie went to the hall with her father. Nate was nowhere to be seen and it took only a few minutes, less than half an hour, for the spokesman to cause uproar among his audience.

'We've great plans to make changes that will benefit everyone in this area,' the spokesman said. 'If everything goes ahead as we hope, we'll be in a position to make all your lives better, so we're looking for your support.'

A man from the audience stood up. 'What plans are you talking about? Why are you back here telling us how you want to change our village? Has Nate Branscombe sold out to you?'

'He hasn't signed the papers yet but our offer is definitely back on the table,' the spokesman answered. He clicked a computer mouse and brought up on the screen in front of them an enlarged photo of their village, nestled in the valley around the beautiful blue bay. 'There's a prime position for a five-star hotel,' he said, pointing to an area on the cliff top to the east. 'Just think how that will boost the prosperity of the area.' He clicked the mouse again. 'And here's the outline of what the proposed shopping mall will look like. There will be restaurants, a leisure centre, a gymnasium, cinema...'

A woman stood up, angrily voicing her

thoughts. 'And along with all that there will be tourists with their cars and takeaway food cartons littering the countryside...broken bottles on the beach... What next—a casino open all hours?'

People stood up, shouting, anxious for their voices to be heard. Some remained seated, Sophie noticed. Not everyone was against change but the majority were adamant that it shouldn't happen, not in their idyllic part of the world.

She left the meeting with her father, taking him back to his home. 'Do you think Nate meant for this to happen?' he asked as she wheeled his chair up the ramp into the house. Charlie woke up from his snooze in the kitchen and came to greet them, tail wagging enthusiastically.

'I don't think so.' She flicked the switch on the kettle. 'But there was some kind of problem—he had to go to see his father's solicitor in London, so I suspect there are financial problems he didn't know about. He hasn't told me anything about it, but I'm guessing it's serious.'

'So you think he'll sell to Peninsula after all?'

'I don't know. I know he doesn't want to.'

Her father was obviously worried as they talked about the possibilities of Peninsula Holdings taking over. 'This place will be the first to go,' he said, looking around the kitchen. 'What are they going to offer me in its place? A ground-floor retirement flat in the suburbs? Their representative seemed to think that would be perfect for me—a place in a warden-assisted block, he said. I could look out on to the street on the front with the shops directly opposite and a communal garden at the back. How would I look after Charlie in a situation like that?'

A look of despair crossed his face. 'I'm used to being in this beautiful place, with trees and shrubs and countryside and the sea not far away, neighbours who pop in to say hello whenever they have five minutes to spare. I can't bear the thought of moving.'

'Perhaps it won't come to that.' She handed him a mug of coffee and slid a plate of his favourite cheese straws towards him. 'I'll go and see Nate—see if he'll talk to me. Maybe together we can come up with some ideas that will help him keep the estate.'

'Bless you, Sophie. I hope there's some way out of the situation.'

The kitchen door opened just then and Jessica came in, wheeling the baby in the pram. Sophie wedged the door open temporarily to allow her into the kitchen and then stopped to coo over the baby. 'Oh, isn't he gorgeous?' He was fast asleep, his little pink hands curled into fists either side of his cheeks. 'He's perfect.'

Jessica smiled. 'He would be if he managed to sleep for more than two hours at a time. I thought if I walked him over here the motion of the pram would rock him to sleep.' She looked down at her baby. 'Oh...I might have known. He's awake again.' She chuckled and carefully lifted him out, wrapping his shawl around him once more. 'I think your grandad wants to see you, young man.'

Her father nodded. 'Oh, definitely. I'll grab my chance to hold him while Rob's spending time down at the beach with his friends. I might not get a look in otherwise.'

'Here you go.' Jessica gently placed Casey in her father's arms. 'Sophie gets to hold him a lot,' she told him with a smile, 'so you get first dibs.'

They sat around the table and talked, taking turns in holding the baby until Charlie began to get restless. He came and laid his head on Sophie's lap, looking at her with big eyes.

Sophie reached for his lead. 'I'll take him out for a walk,' she said. 'Maybe I'll go along the cliff path and up by the Manor. Nate came back from London yesterday, so he might be home. Perhaps I'll get the chance to talk to him.'

'Good idea. Thanks, Sophie.' Her father watched her leave with Charlie. His expression was sad for a moment until he turned back to Jessica and Sophie heard him ask her about Ryan's job and how much longer he would be away.

Sophie loved walking along the cliff top, looking out over the sparkling blue water below. She stood and watched as the waves rolled in to shore, leaving behind bands of white foam and forming rock pools among the shells and pebbles on the sandy beach. Whenever she could, she loved to walk down there, collecting pretty white spiral shells or glossy cowries and periwinkles.

Today, though, she kept to the path and clambered steadily up the hill towards the Manor House. She hoped the gates would be open so that she could simply walk up to the main door, but since the press had taken to bombarding Nate with questions, and generally intruding on his everyday life, he'd taken to using security measures.

She pressed the buzzer and spoke into the intercom. 'It's Sophie,' she said, when Charlotte answered. 'I wondered if I might see Nate.'

'Oh, hello, Sophie.' There was a pause and then she added, 'He says you're to come right in. Is that your dog I can hear alongside you?'

'It is.'

'Ah, he's a lovely dog, is Charlie.' The wrought-iron gates started to swing open and Sophie set out to walk along the long sweeping drive up to the house.

Nate met her halfway. 'Hello, Sophie,' he said. 'It's good to see you.' He hugged her, looking into her eyes with hungry intensity as though he would absorb every part of her. 'I've missed you.'

She clung to him, needing that close, warm contact. 'I missed you too.' She sent him a troubled look. 'I wanted to come and see you before this, but I know you've been busy with family visitors staying over…as well as the business in London. And the press were here a lot, I heard.'

'Yes. Actually, some of them were sympathetic for once, so I spoke to a couple of them briefly. They wanted to concentrate on the fact that I'm a doctor and how it feels to take over the title.'

She smiled. 'There was a beautiful aerial photograph of the Manor House and the estate in one of the national papers.'

'Yes, I saw it. It was a good article too, considering I hadn't given an interview.' He sent her a thoughtful look. 'I was going to come and see you later today—but you've beaten me to it. I expect you're worried about this business with Peninsula?'

'I am. Leastways, my dad's really concerned about what's going to happen.'

'Yes, I guessed as much. I feel bad that you're having to go through all this worry.' He bent down to stroke an eager Charlie and tickle him behind the ears. 'Shall we walk for a while or would you rather go up to the house?'

She smiled. 'I think Charlie would appreciate the walk. I think he was born for the hills and dales—he can go for miles.'

He chuckled. 'Okay. We'll take a stroll by the lake.' He put an arm around her shoulders as they turned on to the perimeter path. It felt good being this close to him, having the warmth of his fingers filter through the fine material of her cashmere top. He pointed out a few changes along the way. 'If you look closely through the trees, you'll see a few log cabins have sprung up here and there. We're still in the process of getting facilities connected—it'll take time, but at least we've made a start.'

She looked at him curiously. 'You're going ahead with your plans, then? I thought everything might have been put on hold when Peninsula started talking about what they wanted to do.'

They were walking through the copse towards the lake, a silver expanse of water bordered by ancient willow trees that dipped their branches gracefully into the water and where spreading oaks mingled with elderberry and blackberry brambles that were luscious with ripening fruit.

'I'll do as much as I can to hold on to the estate, but I'm afraid things are much worse than I realised. Unfortunately, my father hadn't told me the full extent of his liabilities. That's what the solicitor wanted to talk to me about.' He led her to a bench seat set back from the water, close by a landing stage. They sat down and Charlie flopped to the ground at their feet, his tongue hanging out as he panted happily. Sophie looked around. A boat, a small motor launch, was moored by the wooden jetty.

'So the projects you hoped would put things right and cover the debts won't be enough?'

He nodded. 'That's right. My father's financial situation was far worse than he'd said. I think he didn't tell me because he hoped his other investments would come right, but that isn't happening as yet. I'll do what I can to sort out the mess but I'm still working through my options. I've submitted a plan of action to the bank manager and he's going through it with his advisers.'

She reached for his hand and covered his fingers with hers. 'I don't know what to say. I wish there was something I could do to help.'

He smiled. 'It helps just having you by my side, Sophie. I know you're only here because you're worried for your father, but at least I have you for a little while.'

She frowned. 'I don't understand. Why would you say that? I'd be here anyway—don't you know that? I want to be with you.'

'You're seeing Jake, though, aren't you?' A knot formed in his brow. 'There have been rumours. I saw the way you and he acted together on the day of the funeral. He was smiling, relieved almost, after you spoke to him. Up till then I thought I might be in with a chance but after that I realised it could never happen, you and me.'

'Oh, no...I think you misunderstood the situation completely. As to rumours—you know how people get things wrong. They see me having coffee with him in the cafeteria and suddenly it's a full-blown relationship.' She smiled, a small glow starting up inside her. He'd said it—he wanted to be with her. 'There's nothing going on between me and Jake. I told you—we're friends. He was just pleased because I told him someone else is interested in him.'

He drew in a quick stunned breath, his eyes widening.

She said gently, 'I only have feelings for you, Nate. I love you. It's always been you. I just need to hear that you feel the same way towards me.'

He lifted a hand, stroking his thumb lightly across her cheek. 'I wish it were that simple, Sophie.' His eyes darkened, becoming unfathomable like the rippling surface of the lake. 'I love you too, with all my heart, with all my soul, but I can't give in to my feelings for you.'

Anguished, she lifted her hands to his chest, laying her palms flat against the top of his ribcage. 'I don't understand, Nate. I've waited so long to hear you say that you love me. If you feel the same way, why can't we be together?'

He shook his head. 'How can I let it happen when my family has been responsible for so much heartache heaped on your father, on you—perhaps ultimately on everyone who is a part of this estate? My father was responsible for the accident that crippled your father. I can't ever hope to make up for the horror of that.'

'You don't have to…'

'I do.' He straightened. 'I owe you so much but right now I may be about to lose everything I have. Everything I am, my whole existence, my heritage, my family name, is tied up in this place and it's all coming crashing down around me. I can't…I won't…ask you or your family to suffer any more because of my failures. I love you, Sophie, but I can't ask you to be with me, to marry me, until I've restored the family pride and I can offer you the future you deserve.'

She looked at him in shock. 'But I love you, Nate. Isn't that enough to see us through this?

Surely, nothing else matters? We can work this out together, can't we?'

'No, we can't. I'm sorry, Sophie.' He clasped her hands in his. 'When I saw you with Jake, when I didn't see anything of you these last few days, it hit me like a ten-ton truck that I want you more than anything else in the world—I want to be with you, I love you, it's going to be unbearable without you...but I won't put you or your family through any more hardship because of me.'

He kissed her gently, briefly, on the mouth, as though he daren't linger a moment longer for fear of losing himself entirely. Then he stood up. 'I'll walk you back to the gates. Perhaps it's best if we don't see each other for a while.'

Sophie scrambled to her feet and went blindly along beside him. 'You can't do this, Nate. There has to be another way. We can work through this together.'

He didn't answer and that silence made things a hundred times worse. She couldn't feel, couldn't think. She was in shock, her whole body trembling, but she knew there would be no point in trying to speak to him about it any more. He wouldn't talk about it. He had made up his mind and there was nothing she could do to persuade him otherwise.

CHAPTER EIGHT

'YOU'VE JUST COME from the Neonatal Unit again, haven't you?' Hannah smiled as Sophie went over to the coffee machine in the staff lounge. 'I can always tell. Either that or your sister brought the baby in to work to see you.'

'Ah...I can't seem to help myself,' Sophie said, reaching for a mug. 'There's just something about those tiny babies that gets me here, every time.' She pressed the flat of her hand over her heart. 'They're so vulnerable, with tubes for this and that and all the monitoring equipment. I've been doing screening tests today—checking nutrient levels and urea and electrolytes. If there was time, I would spend most of the day in the unit, to be honest.' She smiled. 'But my other patients can be just as adorable. It's so satisfying to see them getting stronger day by day.'

Hannah washed her cup out at the sink. 'I bet you've loved having your sister and her baby staying with you. To look at him you wouldn't think he had such a hard time being born.'

Sophie nodded. 'I've loved every minute of it, and yes, he's doing really well now. He's gaining weight—still not sleeping through the night, of course.'

'Ah—now I know why you've had that peaky look about you of late.' Hannah grinned and started towards the door. 'I'd better get back to work,' she said.

'Okay.' Sophie concentrated on pouring hot coffee into her mug. Peaky? There was only one reason for her being under par lately and that was because of Nate. Why was he so determined that things couldn't work out between them?

'Hi—how are you doing?'

She gave a small start of surprise as she realised Nate had come into the room as Hannah was leaving. The kitchen area was slightly hidden from the entrance. 'Hi. I didn't see you there,' she said as he came to stand alongside her, reaching for a porcelain mug. 'Shall I pour you a coffee?'

'Thanks.'

'How does it feel to be back at work?'

'It feels okay.' He accepted the mug she slid towards him. 'I wasn't sure how it would be, but it's actually good. The chief called me into his office this morning and for a minute I wondered if something was wrong—I was only here on a temporary contract and I'd had to take time off—but he offered me a permanent post.'

Her eyes widened. 'Will you take it?'

He nodded. 'Yes, I like working here. I like the people and the set-up.'

'I'm glad for you.' She sipped her coffee, looking at him over the rim of her cup. 'I suppose at least being here helps take your mind off all your other problems.'

'True.' He searched in the fridge and found a box of doughnuts. 'I brought these in to share out—would you like one?'

'Thanks.' She helped herself, biting into the cake and carefully licking the sugar off her fingers. Nate watched her, as though fascinated by her actions, until he gave himself a shake and put the box back in the fridge.

'So, what's happening with everyone at home?' he asked. 'I feel as though I've been a bit out of touch these last few days while I've been busy trying to sort out problems with the estate.'

'Oh, we're all doing fine. Rob's started a psychology course at college and my dad's doing really well with his physiotherapy. He's taking a few steps on his own now, with the aid of a walking frame. He says he's going to progress from there to walking with elbow crutches.'

'I thought he would manage it, given time. He's always been a determined man. He just needs to strengthen his muscles now.' He studied her. 'I expect Jessica will be going home soon—how will you feel about that? You've enjoyed being with her and the baby, haven't you? I heard you telling Hannah a bit about him.'

Her mouth turned down at the corners. 'I'll hate it when she leaves but Ryan's coming back next week and they'll want to be together in their own home, of course. I'm taking a few days off work to go there with her to help her settle back in... just until Ryan's home.'

'That sounds like a good idea.' He frowned. 'She doesn't like it there, though, does she? She mentioned something to me about it, and I remember you telling me her house is not up to much and there's no garden, just a small yard out back.'

'That's right. It was all they could afford at the time.' She sighed. 'She says she wants to move back to the village. It was where she was born, after all. Ryan's happy to do that but they have to find the right place, somewhere within their budget.'

'Won't Jessica miss your mother if she does that?'

Sophie nodded. 'I'm sure she will...but it's only about an hour away on the train—a bit longer by car. Up to now we've taken it in turns to make the journey, so we all get to see each other at least once a week. It seems to have worked out reasonably well, so far.'

Nate was deep in thought for a minute or two and she looked at him questioningly. 'Is everything all right?'

'Yes, absolutely. I was just wondering whether they might want to live at the Manor. The place is far too big for me. It takes me all my time to use the main part of the house, and then there are the East and the West Wings that can be more or less turned into self-contained units if necessary. If they had part of the East Wing, for instance, they would have access to a terrace and the garden, and there's a kitchen there that used to be the old scullery. They could stay as long as they wanted, make it their home or use it while they build up their finances to get a place of their own.' He sent her a cautious glance. 'What do you think?'

She gasped, her eyes widening. 'What do I think? Oh, Nate!' She flung her arms around his neck and kissed him soundly on the mouth. 'I think you're wonderful, fantastic, beyond words.'

He looked at her in stunned surprise, laughing uncertainly as his hands went automatically around her waist as though they belonged there.

She kissed him again, a longer kiss this time, equally fervent. 'No wonder I love you so much,' she said in a contented whisper. She clung to him, her soft curves crushed against his hard body.

'Sophie...I... We said we wouldn't do this...' He gently tried to push her away but his hands were trembling and the knowledge that he was so affected by her made her blood sizzle with renewed vigour.

'You've got to be kidding,' she said, smiling up at him.

He shook his head, a look of anguish on his face. 'It's too difficult for me if you wrap yourself around me this way,' he said in a distracted, ragged tone. 'I'm only flesh and blood—you're making it way too hard for me to resist you.'

'Good. I'm glad.' She looked at him with sparkling, mischievous eyes. 'It was a silly idea in the first place. Why on earth would you want to keep me away when I can help you get through this awful time? I won't stay away. That's not what love's about, is it? Love is about being there for each other through the hard times. Why should you struggle on your own when I can share your troubles with you? You know what they say—a problem shared is a problem halved?'

'Ah… Sophie…that's not always the case but…' At last he gave in with a small shuddery sigh that seemed to ricochet through his whole body. Joy surged in her at his capitulation, and when he bent his head and rested his forehead against hers, she knew the sweet scent of success. 'I hope you don't come to regret this,' he said huskily. 'Don't say I didn't try to warn you.'

'Yeah, you did…but it didn't work.' She smiled impishly and he kissed her feverishly, with growing passion until she was breathless with longing.

They came up for air just as they heard the door open and someone came into the room. By the time Tracey came over to the coffee machine and saw them there, they had managed to compose themselves once more.

'Oh, hi there,' Tracey said, pausing to look in the fridge. 'Did I hear there were doughnuts to be had?'

'There certainly are—in the white box.' Nate

smiled at her. 'They say an army marches on its stomach. I think the same goes for hospital staff— we can't work properly if we're hungry.'

Tracey laughed and bit into the doughnut. 'Mmm...delicious. Just what I needed.' She looked at Nate. 'I saw an article on the Manor House in the paper the other day—the photo that went alongside it was beautiful with the sun glowing on the stonework...and the stable block at the back through the courtyard...and the grounds looked so lush. I can't imagine living in a place like that...I'd never want to come in to work— I'd want to go out and explore it every day. It makes me think how it might have been in Regency times—peaceful and perfect and genteel.'

'There is that, I suppose.' Nate thought about it. 'There are portraits of the ancestors in the West Wing—women in their ballgowns or day dresses, and the men rigged out in their finery. I take it for granted, probably, and I tend not to think about it too much—I'm too busy trying to be a doctor.'

'Yes...I can see you have your priorities sorted.' Tracey smiled and helped herself to coffee while

Sophie and Nate excused themselves and prepared to go back to the Children's Unit.

'You didn't send the ancestral portraits to auction, then?' Sophie said quietly as they walked along the corridor. 'I saw some of the paintings being collected one day when I was walking Charlie.'

He shook his head. 'No, only some that I really didn't like. Quite a few were stored in the attic and hadn't seen the light of day for many years. The proceeds will go towards the work on the fishing lodges.'

She glanced at him. 'You know, Tracey may have come up with something when she mentioned the Regency period of the Manor House. You often get film companies or TV production companies wanting to use historic houses as locations. It might be worth thinking of that as an option. I don't know whether it would make much of a difference to your situation.'

To her surprise, he nodded. 'Actually, ever since that picture appeared in the paper I've been receiving requests from companies interested in using the property. I wasn't sure how much of a disruption it would be—but I'm told it would be the ideal location for a TV drama series set in the mid-nineteenth century, and also there's a company looking to make a period adventure film with a grand mansion at its centre. I'm not sure. They won't need to use the whole house, but they're happy that there's plenty of space for the trucks and equipment. They won't be there for too long, I imagine. What do you think?'

Her eyes widened. 'I think it sounds really exciting, and I can't see too many problems as long as you're dealing with companies that have good reputations. I think you need to give it some deep thought. It's your home, after all.' She frowned. 'Perhaps you could persuade them to keep the disruption to a minimum—have them use separate entrances, maybe? And I guess the vehicles might be hidden by the trees and shrubs if they used the West side of the house. What matters is that you feel comfortable with your decision.'

'Thanks, Sophie. I knew you would put it all into perspective for me.' He put his arm around her and briefly hugged her. 'You're right. I need to give it a lot of thought.'

They went their separate ways, attending to their small patients. Sophie's mind was buzzing with questions yet to be answered as she checked lab reports and studied X-ray films and CT scans. What would he decide?

Sophie was away from home for the next few days, so she didn't get the chance to be with him and work through the choices he might make. Instead, she helped Jessica get her house organised and pristine once more after the boiler and central-heating repairs.

'I can hardly believe Nate is being so generous, offering us a place in his home,' Jessica said excitedly. 'I talked to Ryan about it on the phone and he thinks it's a great idea…though, with all the business of the film-company offer and so on, Nate probably has too much on his mind. He might have had second thoughts about it.'

Sophie shook her head. 'No, he called me this morning and said you can move in whenever you want.' She looked at the baby lying in his cradle. He opened his eyes and looked at her, making little gurgling sounds and blowing tiny bubbles from his perfect mouth. Sophie lightly stroked his soft palm and he gripped her fingers tightly in response. She smiled down at him. 'Nate said there's a room that can be turned into a nursery,' she told Jessica. 'You just need to let him know how you want it decorated and he'll get things organised.'

'Oh, I can't wait!'

Ryan came home next day and Sophie left the two of them to spend time together with their baby. She arrived home and a bit later she went over to her father's house, to find him and Rob preparing for another meeting at the Manor. It was Friday evening and Nate had phoned her earlier to make sure she would be able to come along.

'He's invited all the villagers from the estate, plus any others who are interested in knowing what he plans to do,' her father said. 'Do you know what he has in mind?'

She shook her head. 'I don't. He was sifting through various options, talking with the bank manager and so on, last time I spoke to him about it.' She looked at her father, spruce in a dark grey suit and shiny polished shoes. 'You're looking very smart,' she said. 'It's not a formal do, is it? Nate didn't mention anything like that.' She was a bit concerned that she might not be dressed for the occasion. She was wearing a soft wool dress with a slightly off-the-shoulder neckline and three-quarter sleeves. It was comfortable and classic and she felt good in it.

Her father laughed. 'No, it isn't a formal do… I just wanted to celebrate being able to get out of the wheelchair and stand up for a while. See?' He stood up carefully, taking his time, and Rob came over to him and handed him a couple of elbow crutches.

'One step at a time, Dad,' he said. 'Remember how we practised this…'

Sophie watched as her father slowly walked across the room, straight-backed and proud. 'Oh, Dad,' she cried, going over to him. 'It's wonderful. I'm so happy for you.' She hugged him, and hugged her brother. 'Now look what you've both done,' she said, choked up. 'I'm all tearful and at this rate I'll have to do my make-up all over again!'

They both laughed and a few minutes later they all set off for the Manor House.

Nate greeted them and showed them into the long panelled room where everyone was assembled, helping themselves to refreshments. There was a variety of food, as before, with southern fried chicken, spring rolls and salsa dips, and a range of desserts that included strawberry bruschetta and dishes of Eton mess.

Nate drew Sophie to him and dropped a kiss on her mouth. 'I'm really glad you're back,' he said, grabbing her hand and leading her over to the side of the room where a bar had been set up. He handed her a glass of wine and murmured, 'I have to go and talk to everyone—help yourself to food and sit down close by me, will you? It's good to have you here. I can't tell you how much I worried while you were away. I thought you might have changed your mind about us, knowing what might lie ahead.'

She looked at him thoughtfully. 'You're still worried I might disappear out of your life?'

He moved his shoulders awkwardly. 'I wanted so much for things to work out for us. I hardly dared hope...'

'You know I'll be here for you, always. The way I feel won't ever change, Nate.'

He exhaled slowly and gently squeezed her fingers. 'I'm glad. Hearing you say it makes me feel so much better.' He braced himself. 'Here goes, then.'

He called for everyone to take a seat, and when they were settled, he said, 'Thank you for coming here today. I know you've all been worried about what might happen to the estate...to your homes. I'm here to tell you what's been decided and how we'll be going forward from now on. None of it involves Peninsula Holdings. I turned their offer down and they won't be coming back.'

A cheer went up and he smiled. 'Yes, I thought you would like that. But I have accepted a couple of other offers that might affect you in a round-about way. I've agreed to let a TV company use the West Wing of the Manor House in order to make a period drama series, and I've also signed an agreement to allow a film company to use the house at a later date.'

There were gasps of astonishment from the villagers and a buzz of excited conversation started up. People started asking questions and Nate held his hand up for quiet. 'I know there are things you want to ask,' he said, 'and there will be time for that. Let me just say that the activities of the companies will take a matter of months and there shouldn't be any impact on the village—apart from perhaps a few more customers in the shops or the pub for a while.'

'Will we get a visit from Colin Firth?' one woman called out hopefully.

'Does Daniel Craig do period drama?' another asked with a wistful expression.

Sophie laughed, and Nate smiled. 'I wouldn't know about that,' he said. 'All I want to say, to finish, is that your houses are safe and you need have no worries for the future on that account.'

Everyone started talking at once and Sophie

took a moment to quietly say to him, 'Has it really solved all of your problems? Are you out of the woods now?'

He nodded. 'Oh, yes,' he said. 'They're paying me an embarrassing amount of money—a lot of it up front, so I can categorically say the future's looking rosy.'

She laid a hand on his arm, her fingers curling around his sleeve. 'I'm so happy for you. I know how much all this means to you.'

'It means everything to me to know that your father's house is safe and his way of life won't be disrupted any more. He's doing so well, isn't he? And you and I... Now we can have a future together, can't we, Sophie?'

'We always could,' she said. 'You know I don't need a Manor House and all the trappings of an estate to keep me happy. I just want you—the man who saves a little boy's life when he collapses in the street, or feeds a baby in Neonatal—the man who brings my sister to me and gives my brother a lift late at night. You're everything I want, Nate.'

He bent his head to her and kissed her. 'I can't

wait for everyone to go,' he said under his breath. 'I want you all to myself.'

She chuckled and went with him to mingle with the crowd and answer questions about the TV production and his plans for the estate.

Her father hugged her as he said goodbye a while later. 'You and Nate are obviously very happy with one another,' he said. 'I'm pleased for you. Does your mother know?'

'I mentioned it to her when I went over to Jessica's house. She seemed to accept it. I think she'll be happy as long as you're happy with it.'

He nodded. 'I'll give her a call.'

He and Rob left to go home, and gradually the rest of the villagers began to take their leave. Nate and Sophie saw them off, and when the last one had gone, Nate gave a soft sigh of relief.

'Come into the drawing room with me,' he said, taking Sophie by the hand and leading her into a room off the wide hallway. 'I have something for you.'

Sophie looked around. She remembered this room from before, with its pale silk wall coverings, cream sofas and luxurious oriental rug. The curtains were drawn now, beautiful brocade drapes that elegantly skirted the floor. Several lamps were lit in here, casting a golden glow over the room, and the wood-burning stove flickered with gentle heat in the inglenook fireplace.

Nate went over to a bureau in the corner of the room. He took a small box from a drawer and turned to her. 'I wanted to give you this,' he said, going over to where she stood in the middle of the room and getting down on one knee in front of her. He carefully opened the box to reveal an exquisite sparkling diamond ring nestled on a bed of silk. Brilliant light was reflected from every perfect facet.

Sophie gasped. 'Oh, Nate...'

'Will you marry me, Sophie?' he asked. 'Will you accept this ring as a token of my love and as my promise that I will always be yours?'

'Oh, Nate...yes.' Her voice broke with emotion. 'I will. I'm overwhelmed.'

He exhaled slowly as though he'd been holding his breath in preparation for her answer. He stood up and placed the box on a table, taking out the ring and turning towards her once more. He reached for her left hand and carefully slid the ring on to her finger. 'It fits perfectly, doesn't it?' he said. 'I asked Jessica your ring size.'

'Ah...that's how you knew. Yes, it does... Wait till I see her—she didn't say a word to me about this! Nate, it's so beautiful.' She looked at him, her eyes shining with happiness.

'It's where it belongs—on your finger. There's a wedding ring made to go with it. Perhaps we could make it a short engagement? I know it's traditional to have a summer wedding, but I was thinking maybe Christmas would be a good time? We could be married in the village church and then come back here for the celebrations. What do you think?'

She lifted her arms to him and wound them lightly around his neck. 'I think that sounds wonderful,' she said.

He wrapped his hands around her waist and drew her to him. 'We could honeymoon in the

Caribbean, after the festivities. Do you think you would like that?'

'Anywhere would be lovely,' she murmured, 'as long as I'm with you.'

He smiled and kissed her tenderly, with growing passion. 'I've a feeling that life is going to be sheer bliss from now on,' he said after a while, his voice roughened.

She came up for air briefly. 'Oh, yes, definitely.' She kissed him again and neither of them spoke for a long, long time after that. They were far too busy showing their love for one another.

* * * * *

If you enjoyed this story, check out these other great reads from Joanna Neil

HER HOLIDAY MIRACLE
RESISTING HER REBEL DOC
TEMPTATION IN PARADISE
DARING TO DATE HER BOSS

All available now!

MILLS & BOON®
Large Print Medical

May

The Nurse's Christmas Gift	Tina Beckett
The Midwife's Pregnancy Miracle	Kate Hardy
Their First Family Christmas	Alison Roberts
The Nightshift Before Christmas	Annie O'Neil
It Started at Christmas...	Janice Lynn
Unwrapped by the Duke	Amy Ruttan

June

White Christmas for the Single Mum	Susanne Hampton
A Royal Baby for Christmas	Scarlet Wilson
Playboy on Her Christmas List	Carol Marinelli
The Army Doc's Baby Bombshell	Sue MacKay
The Doctor's Sleigh Bell Proposal	Susan Carlisle
Christmas with the Single Dad	Louisa Heaton

July

Falling for Her Wounded Hero	Marion Lennox
The Surgeon's Baby Surprise	Charlotte Hawkes
Santiago's Convenient Fiancée	Annie O'Neil
Alejandro's Sexy Secret	Amy Ruttan
The Doctor's Diamond Proposal	Annie Claydon
Weekend with the Best Man	Leah Martyn